GHOST MOON

JOHN WILSON

GHOST MOON

ORCA BOOK PUBLISHERS

Text copyright © 2011 John Wilson

Library and Archives Canada Cataloguing in Publication

Wilson, John (John Alexander), 1951-
Ghost moon / John Wilson.

Issued also in electronic formats.
ISBN 978-1-55469-879-0

I. Title.
PS8595.I5834G55 2011   JC813'.54   C2011-903511-1

First published in the United States, 2011
Library of Congress Control Number: 2011907455

Summary: In the late 1870s, young Jim Doolen travels to New Mexico, where he befriends
Bill Bonney and ends up in the middle of the Lincoln County War.

MIX
Paper from
responsible sources
FSC® C016245
www.fsc.org

*Orca Book Publishers is dedicated to preserving the environment and has printed this book
on paper certified by the Forest Stewardship Council®.*

Orca Book Publishers gratefully acknowledges the support for its publishing programs
provided by the following agencies: the Government of Canada through the Canada Book
Fund and the Canada Council for the Arts, and the Province of British Columbia through
the BC Arts Council and the Book Publishing Tax Credit.

Cover design by Teresa Bubela
Cover photo by John Wilson
Author photo by Katherine Gordon

ORCA BOOK PUBLISHERS
PO Box 5626, Stn. B
Victoria, BC Canada
V8R 6S4

ORCA BOOK PUBLISHERS
PO Box 468
Custer, WA USA
98240-0468

www.orcabook.com
Printed and bound in Canada.

14 13 12 11 • 4 3 2 1

For Shaun and Petra, with thanks for the many April visits.

It is time for you to go, Busca. The ghost moon is full."

It's morning, and Wellington and I are sitting on the ledge outside his cave eating a breakfast of tortillas and beans. A light breeze is sending tiny whirlwinds of dust across the flat ledge before us. "What's a ghost moon?" I ask my old friend.

Wellington waves his arm in the direction of the pale, silver globe hanging in the washed-out blue sky above the dark brown hills to the east. "*La luna,*" he says. "The moon is the poor cousin of the sun. Her job is to brighten the night, but she's jealous of her relative who gives so much light and warmth in the day.

Every month, the moon tries as hard as she can to be as bright as her cousin. She almost succeeds, but the effort is too much and she fades away, only to try once more the next month.

"Sometimes, when the moon is full, she thinks that this time she will become as bright as her cousin. When she is arrogant like this, the sun decides to teach her a lesson and invites her to a competition during the daylight. Of course, the poor moon always loses this competition, as you see." Wellington indicates the moon once more. "*La luna del fantasma*, the ghost moon."

"It does look as if you can see through it," I agree.

"It is well to know one's place in the world, Busca. The moon has no place in the day."

I've enjoyed my days with Wellington and Perdido, the mummified conquistador who sits in my friend's cave, telling the story of my adventures at Casas Grandes and listening to his stories of scouting with the army and escorting English hunters. But he's right, ghost moon or not, it's time for me to move on.

After Casas Grandes, I returned to Esqueda, where I spent Christmas with Santiago having my broken ribs tended to by his mad wife, Maria. It was a wonderfully relaxing time with no danger and nothing to do but write letters to my mother back in Yale and read *Moby Dick*.

However, by the third week of January, I was becoming restless. It was time to head up to Lincoln and find work, and, on the way, keep my promise to Wellington to return and tell him how my story turned out. I saddled Coronado, and we retraced our route north to Wellington and Perdido's cave.

"It is time for me to go," I agree with Wellington.

My friend nods. "You are a seeker, Busca. Now that you have discovered your father, what do you seek next?"

"I'll head over to Lincoln County. I've heard there's work there and money to be made."

Wellington snorts disparagingly. "In my experience, Busca, wherever there is money to be made, *apuro*, trouble always follows close behind."

"I don't mind," I say with a shrug. "I want to learn about the world and have adventures."

"I envy you your youth and enthusiasm, but remember this, Busca: to learn from your adventures, you must first survive them. You were lucky on the trail to Esqueda. Next time it might not be Nah-kee-tats-an who finds you. My people are restless. Many prefer the hardships of living free in the mountains to accepting food from the government on the reservations. I should be sad to see your scalp hanging from a warrior's lance."

I begin to protest that I'll be fine, but Wellington holds up his hand to stop me. "Do not argue with me," he says with a smile. "I know you will do what you must. Just as Perdido and I did when we were young men. Just as Nah-kee-tats-an does today."

Wellington falls silent and stares at the moon. I am about to collect my bedroll and go and find Coronado, when he stirs. "Did you read the book I gave you about the great white whale?"

I'm a little bit taken aback by the question and hesitate for a moment before answering. "I read it in Esqueda," I say. "It's a good story."

"It's a long story. I think your story is like that. It is not finished yet."

I have no idea where Wellington is going with this, but I know him well enough to know he has some point to make. I sit in silence and eventually he continues. "I have been having many dreams lately. You are in them, and so is Nah-kee-tats-an. I think the spirits are telling me that your futures are intertwined."

I can't imagine how they might be. The last time I saw Nah-kee-tats-an, he was heading east to join Victorio. I doubt very much if he'll come to Lincoln.

"But perhaps that is not what my dreams mean," Wellington goes on. "I am in these dreams as well.

I sit with Perdido in our cave. He tells me that times are changing and that the world does not need old men like us anymore. He says we must leave this place and go our own ways. Then he gets up and goes out of the cave. I follow him, but he dissolves to dust in the sunlight. I turn back, but my cave is gone, replaced by a wide plain. On the plain are a lake and a large building of stone. I think it is a castle like the ones that the Englishman, Lord Alfred George Cambrey Sommerville, Earl of Canterbury, told me about, but it is a ruin. There is a battle raging over the ruins, but I cannot see who is fighting. There are many bodies on the ground and much blood. A voice in my head tells me I must leave this place, but where am I to go? I walk away."

"What does it mean?"

Wellington shrugs. "*No sé.* I do not know, but I am certain that I must leave my cave. Am I to accompany you to Lincoln?"

"I don't think so," I say too hurriedly. I've been looking forward to being on my own again. Fond as I am of Wellington, I can't see me arriving in Lincoln looking for work with an aged Apache in tow.

Wellington surprises me by laughing. "Your face is like the page of a book, Busca. Youth does not wish to be tethered to age. I shall leave here, but not with you. Perhaps I am to go and fight with Nah-kee-tats-an. Did you know that he is my son?"

"I guessed from talking with him. But you're too old to fight," I blurt out rudely.

Again Wellington laughs. "Youth thinks life ends when the first wrinkle appears on the skin or the first ache troubles a joint. You do not know Kas-tziden, known to you white men as Nana?"

I shake my head.

"You would have called him old when he fought with Mangas Coloradas and Cochise, and was married to Geronimo's sister. Now he is older even than me. Some say he has seen more than eighty winters. Yet he fights alongside the young warriors in the Sierra Madre Mountains. Youth is not everything."

"I'm sorry," I say. "I did not mean to insult you."

"You do not insult me," Wellington says, the smile still on his face. "But you cannot help me interpret my dreams. Do not worry. I shall not trouble you with my company. And I shall not run to the hills to fight. Not yet. I shall dream and sit by my cave, discussing the world and what it means with Perdido, until things become clear. You must follow your story and find your adventures. But take care. These are troubled times, and there are many traps set out to snare us. This is a land of many legends. You are making your own legends, but you cannot escape those around you, both the legends of the past and the ones others make. We do not always have control over our stories, and they do not always take us where we would like or intend to go. I wish you luck, Busca."

"I hope you find the answer to your dreams," I say, standing.

Wellington nods distractedly. He has finished saying what he needs to and gazes over the landscape, contemplating other things. I gather my belongings, leave what is left of the sacks of flour and beans I brought up with me and bid farewell to Perdido. Wellington doesn't even look up as I set off down the hillside to where Coronado waits for me. Despite what Wellington has said about these being troubled times, I am happy, excited to be on the trail once more and thrilled by what the future might hold.

"**G**host moon," the kid repeats. "That's a good name. Sure ain't the bright ball that gave me enough light to build a fire, brew coffee and pack up this morning afore dawn. My ma used to call the full moon in daylight a lace moon, 'cause it looks just like one of those round pieces of lace you set on the table when company's coming."

It's three days since I left Wellington's cave. I broke camp early this morning, figuring that if I got a good start on the trail, I could make Lincoln in enough time to look for work in the short February daylight. I ran into the kid almost immediately, heading up from the south. I kept my hand on my revolver as he approached, but he didn't seem to be any kind of a threat, waving a greeting and shouting hello when he was still some distance away.

He introduced himself as Bill Bonney, but said that everyone just calls him Kid because he's only eighteen. That makes him two years older than me, but he's smooth-cheeked and lightly built and could pass for younger. I think back to the other Kid I've met—the man I killed last year. But Bill is different. I've immediately taken a liking to him. He's cheerful and has a fresh, open face and a ready gap-toothed smile. His eyes are a striking hazel color, and he wears his light brown hair long and carefully groomed.

"Lace moon," I say. "That's a good name for it too. Where's your ma now?"

"Who knows. Where d'you reckon we go after we die?"

"I'm sorry," I say, feeling my face flush with embarassment.

Bill shrugs. "No need. It weren't no surprise. The white plague, consumption some call it, kills slow. That's why we moved out west to Colorado and then down here to New Mexico. The dry air's good for the lungs. Not good enough though. Ma's been dead four years."

"Your dad still alive?" I ask, thinking about all I discovered about my father and the mysterious life he led.

"My da," the kid says, a touch of Irish brogue appearing in his voice. "Which da d'you mean? I've had a couple." Before I can think of a response, the kid continues. "My real da, Michael McCarty, came over from Ireland on the coffin ships after the famine. So did my ma, Catherine, though they didn't meet till they were both in New York. That's where I was born, me and my brother Joe. I don't remember much of them days. My da was killed in the New York draft riots in '63. I were but a nipper, no more'n four years old. Can't say as I remember him much.

"Ma said that his death were a godsend, that Da was getting into a lot of bad stuff, drinking, fighting, hanging out with the Dead Rabbits Gang around Five Points."

"Dead Rabbits Gang?" I ask.

Bill laughs. "Sounds funny, don't it, but they weren't. And they had little to do with rabbits, except when they went into a fight with another gang. Then they carried a dead rabbit on a pole like a battle flag. *Rabbit* were from an Irish word, *ráibéad*. It means someone to be frightened of, and *dead* means very. So, a dead rabbit was someone to be greatly feared." Bill suddenly throws his head back and bursts into song:

"They had a dreadful fight, upon last Saturday night,
The papers gave the news accordin';
Guns, pistols, clubs and sticks, hot water and
  old bricks,
Which drove them on the other side of Jordan.

Then pull off the coat and roll up the sleeve,
For Bayard is a hard street to travel;
So pull off the coat and roll up the sleeve,
The Bloody Sixth is a hard ward to travel, I believe."

Bill's voice is deeper than I expect from his skinny frame, and he can hold a tune well. He finishes singing and grins broadly at me. "That's all my da left me, a song about a street fight in New York." His face becomes serious. "Ma said that if my da hadn't been killed, he would've dragged me and Joe down with him.

"As it were, Ma moved us out to Indianapolis, where she met and married William Henry Harrison Antrim. Mouthful of a name, eh?"

"It is," I agree, "but if your real father was called McCarty and your stepfather was called Antrim, why are you called Bonney?"

Bill laughs. "And why am I called Bill when I were christened Henry? Henry McCarty, Henry Antrim,

Kid, Kid Antrim, I been 'em all. William's my second given name, and Bonney's just the latest surname. You read much?"

"Some," I say, surprised by the question.

"Dime novels?"

"Sure, I've read a lot of dime novels, about Kit Carson, Davy Crockett, the Alamo."

"'The valley of the Mississippi River, from its earliest settlement, has been more infested with reckless and bloodstained men than any other part of the country.'"

"I know that," I say as realization dawns. "It's the beginning of *Murderer's Doom* by Edward Bonney. You took a dime novelist's name."

"Why not?" Bill says. "Name don't mean nothing. Just a flag by which folks know you, and sometimes"—he winks broadly at me—"it pays to change what folks know you as."

I don't agree with Bill, or whatever he's called. Names have been very important to some of the people I've met. To Wellington and Nah-kee-tats-an, and to me, James Doolen, or Busca, in my search for my father. But my companion's laugh is infectious, and I can't help smiling along with him. "Where's your second dad now?" I ask. "Is he still alive?"

"He's alive all right. Prospecting over by the Arizona Territory border, around Silver City. That's where I been, visiting my da."

Bill's brow furrows at the memory. "You got no right to ask all them questions and go prying into a fella's past." The sudden anger in his voice startles me. But before I can respond, he spurs his horse ahead, leaving me to reflect.

For a while I stare at Bill's back, confused by his abrupt change in mood. He's wearing a faded blue army jacket over a collarless shirt and a heavy wool vest. There's a battered Mexican sombrero on his head and a fine-looking gray horse beneath him. He carries a Winchester '73 rifle in a scabbard by his saddle and a revolver that I don't recognize in a holster on his right hip. Bill has told me he works on a ranch outside Lincoln. But he's not dressed like a cowboy and carries no lariat. I wonder what kind of work he does.

We are riding a narrow trail over bare scrub hills. There's a chill in the desert air, and I'm wearing a thick poncho that Santiago gave me. It doubles as a blanket at night. Lincoln can't be far ahead, and I wonder what I'll find there. Work and adventure, I hope. And perhaps a letter from my mother in Yale, although I doubt she's had time to reply to my letters from Esqueda yet.

All of a sudden, Bill reins in and turns to face me. He's smiling again and his mood has swung back to jovial companionability as quickly as it descended into anger. "There she is," he says, waving an arm over the valley below.

I draw up beside him and look down. The valley is narrow between the dry hills, and a meandering line of trees marks the course of the Rio Bonita. A two-story adobe building dominates the town and dwarfs the handful of other stores and houses scattered along the single street. Five or six small homesteads are scattered farther off over the valley floor.

"That's Lincoln?" I ask, astonished at its small size.

Bill laughs out loud. "Impressive, ain't it? But don't be fooled. See that large building surrounded by the fence?" I nod. "That's the Murphy House. From the parlor in there, Jimmy Dolan controls most of this entire county. Lawrence Murphy's his partner, but he's a drooling, drunken idiot. Won't live the year out, I reckon.

"Dolan's the power in the whole county. His store supplies everyone from the smallest homesteader to the army post up the river at Fort Stanton, and from the poorest Apache on the reservation at Tularosa to the richest cattle rancher. And he ain't afraid to charge top dollar, neither."

Bill stops and stares hard at me. "You ain't related to Dolan, are you?"

It takes me a moment to work out what he means. "No," I say. "My name's Doolen. It sounds a bit the same, but I'm not related to anyone called Dolan."

Bill nods, apparently satisfied.

"This Dolan"—I emphasize the *o* to make sure Bill can't confuse it with the *oo* in my name—"he has no competition?" I ask.

"Ah, now," Bill replies, his Irish lilt returning, "there's the question. You see that stone tower on Main Street?" He points down into the valley. If I squint, I can make out a round tower down the street from the Murphy House. "That's the *torreón*, built for refuge when the wild Apache's attacked. Farther along, that low building with the veranda over the boardwalk out front. That's John Tunstall's store. He runs it with Alex McSween. Beside it, the house shaped like a U, that's McSween's house."

"That's Dolan's competition?" I ask.

"Sure is, and they'll be your new bosses if you want to work."

"I do."

Bill nods, turns his horse's head and trots off along the crest of the ridge. "Aren't we going into town?" I shout after him.

"Wouldn't want to do that," the kid replies over his shoulder. "Unless you want to work for Mr. Dolan." I shake my head. "Then John Tunstall's spread is some thirty miles southeast on the Rio Feliz. That's where the work is."

With a last look at Lincoln, I turn and follow Bill, who has begun whistling a jaunty dance tune. As I stare at his back, I wonder who my new friend is. He's charming, no doubt, and clever and entertaining. But he reminds me of one of those African lizards I've read about. The ones that can change color to blend in with their environment. Bill's like that—one minute cheerful and singing, the next sullen and angry. In one breath he sounds like a happy Irish layabout. In the next, he's a rough cowboy. Who is he, and where is he leading me?

"Bill! Where in great heaven have you been?"
The tall thin man steps forward from his two companions and shouts to us in a refined English accent as soon as we are within earshot. He doesn't look much older than Bill and me. He's well dressed in a high-collar jacket, open at the neck to reveal a clean white shirt and red necktie.

"I been visiting my da, Mr. Tunstall," Bill replies. "I told you afore I was going."

"Right enough, you did," Tunstall acknowledges. He wears his brown hair slicked back with oil and sports a thin growth of beard around his chin. We dismount as we reach the gate. "And you've brought

17

us another companion," he says, stepping forward and extending a pale hand. "John Henry Tunstall, late of Hackney in England and more recently of the colony of British Columbia in Canada. Pleased to make your acquaintance."

"Jim Doolen," I reply, clasping the offered hand, "also of British Columbia."

"Indeed? Whereabouts?" His grip is firm, and his eyes regard me with studied interest.

"Yale. My mother runs the stopping house there."

"Yale. I have passed through there," Tunstall says cheerfully. "Unfortunately, I did not take the opportunity to avail myself of your family's hospitality. I was located in the fine city of Victoria. I ran the London Emporium on Wharf Street."

"I've been there!" I exclaim, excitedly. "My mother took me to Victoria once on the steamer. We visited the Emporium. She bought several bolts of cloth, I recall. There was everything in that store."

Tunstall laughs at my enthusiasm. "I suppose it must have appeared like a wonderland compared to the stores in Yale. It is indeed a small world we find ourselves in, young Jim. Would I be correct in assuming that you are here in Bill's company to seek gainful employment?"

"Yes, sir," I say.

"Then you have it. We need all the good men we can find, and I shall enjoy many hours talking with you about the common ground we share."

One of the men behind Tunstall coughs pointedly.

"But I fear that must await quieter times. Allow me to introduce my companions. My partner in business, Alexander McSween. Keep in well with him, he's a lawyer and will tie you in knots faster than you can blink an eye." One of the two men steps forward and shakes my hand. He is older than Tunstall, with deep-set eyes, dark receding hair and a drooping mustache that makes him appear to be frowning. "Welcome" is all he says.

"And this is my foreman, Dick Brewer. He may look young, but there is precious little this man does not know about cattle." Brewer shakes my hand and nods. He has a pleasant, open face, a strong chin and a ready smile. He's the only one of the three dressed in work clothes.

"I'm afraid conditions here are a touch crude." Tunstall waves at a small log cabin, the only building I can see. "Yonder stands my mansion." He laughs. "I have built a more commodious dwelling in the town of Lincoln, and one day a fine ranch house will stand here. But for now we must make do. You do not object to bedding beneath the stars?"

"Not at all," I reply.

"Excellent. I think you shall do splendidly here, young Jim. Well, I will let Bill show you around. Tomorrow we run a small herd of horses up to Lincoln, and you must come along to see some of the country and what we face here."

Tunstall and the other two turn away and begin talking earnestly. Bill leads me over to the corral, where we unsaddle our mounts, water them and hitch them to the rough fence. Then we head over to a campsite where some crude lean-tos are scattered around a large fire pit.

"It ain't the St. Francis Hotel in Santa Fe," Bill says, throwing his saddlebags under one of the lean-tos and laying his Winchester beside them, "but you're welcome to share."

"Thank you," I say, laying out my bedroll. "Mr. Tunstall seems like a good man."

"He is that," Bill says. "Always treated me well enough. I just hope he ain't taken on too much."

"What do you mean?"

"I guess I'd best tell you something of what's going on here if'n you're going to ride into the hornet's nest with us tomorrow." Bill sits by his bedroll, and I step over to join him. "Tunstall and that lawyer fella, McSween, aim to go up against Dolan for a share of the commerce in this county, army contracts and so forth."

"That's good, isn't it?" I say. "Must be plenty of business for both."

"There's plenty business all right, but Dolan don't want to give it up. You see, he ain't just a storekeep; he's supported by a bunch of big businessmen up in Santa Fe. And they got most every lawman, judge and politician in the county in their pocket. They take a cut of Dolan's profit, and in exchange they keep everyone else out and keep Dolan's profits high. Dolan keeps his prices expensive and that hurts the small homesteaders and the Hispanics. That's why most of them support Tunstall. On top of that, Tunstall and McSween have taken a couple of army contracts and that hurts Dolan."

"But what can Dolan do about it?"

Bill tilts his head and stares at me. "You ain't been around much, have you?" he asks.

I'm stung by his question, but I have to admit he's right. I saw and did a lot down in Mexico, but all this talk of crooked judges and politicians and business dealings is foreign to me.

"I'm not a businessman," I say defensively.

Bill lets out a short laugh. "And that ain't what you're being hired for. Let me see that pistol you carry."

I hand over the Colt Pocket revolver that my mother gave me when I left Yale. Bill turns it in his hand and expertly opens it and checks the chambers. He nods approvingly. "So you know enough to keep the chamber under the hammer empty so as not to shoot yourself in the foot by accident. But it's an old gun—single action and cap and ball loading. Not the best in a fight."

"My father said that if you need more than two shots, you're probably already dead."

"He's right enough there," Bill says seriously, "if you're up against one man. But if you're in a gunfight against five or six, you need to fire and reload quick." He hands me back my gun and pulls his revolver from its holster. I immediately recognize the prancing horse on the handle. "This here's brand-new last year from Mr. Colt. Sales fella called it the 'New .41 caliber, double-action, self-cocking, central-fire six-shot revolver,' but most just know it as the Thunderer. You don't need to take the cylinder out to reload."

Bill pops open a section of the revolver to expose the right side of the cylinder. He pulls back a button below the barrel and the bullet pops out. He twirls it in his finger and pops it back in, closing the section with a click.

"Easy," he says with a smile.

"Yes," I agree, "but isn't it the same action as the Peacemaker?"

"It is," Bill says, "but the Peacemaker's single action. You have to cock the hammer each time between shots. This beauty's double action—cocks itself so it'll fire as fast as you can pull the trigger."

Despite what my father said, I'm impressed. I doubt I would stand much chance against someone armed with one of these.

"Ever killed a man?" Bill's question takes me by surprise. I have, but I don't like to think about it. I rationalize that the Kid I ambushed was killed when his head hit the rock, and Ed and his companion died in the heat of battle when Nah-kee-tats-an and I were fighting for our lives. I never had a choice. I've never deliberately killed anyone. Have I? I'm not a killer. Nevertheless, I nod in answer.

Bill laughs loudly. "Well. Well. There's more to you than meets the eye, young Jim Doolen. Maybe a hardened killer like yourself needs a nickname. How about the Canada Kid?"

"No," I say more loudly than I intend.

"Okay." Bill throws up his hands in mock surrender. "No nicknames, killer."

"Have *you* ever killed a man?" I ask aggressively.

Bill's smile fades. "It were over in Camp Grant this summer past." Bill has slipped into his cowboy drawl. "Me and a couple of boys had got into trouble for borrowing horses that we didn't rightly own. One night I was in the cantina, and this big fella, Windy Cahill, the local blacksmith, starts roughing me up, calling me a horse thief and all. Now, I fought back, but Cahill were huge. He could near enough pick me up in one hand. I had no choice. I shot him and ran. I heard later that he were gut shot and died screaming that night."

Bill falls silent. His story makes sense and sounds like self-defence. After a minute, he looks up at me and smiles. "So we're both killers," he says, standing up. "Come on, let's get the fire going afore the boys get in from herding."

I follow Bill over to the fire pit, deep in thought. He's right, we have both killed men, but Bill and I are different. I've spent hours awake at night feeling guilt at what I've done, even though the men I've killed were trying to kill me. Bill doesn't seem to feel that way. I couldn't help noticing a note of pride in his voice when he was relating the story of shooting Cahill. Once more, I wonder what I'm getting into.

“Those are good-looking horses, Mr. Tunstall.” I am riding beside Bill and Tunstall behind the nine horses we are herding up to Lincoln to sell. Brewer and four other hands are scattered around the herd.

“Thank you,” Tunstall says. “A horse makes living in this land possible. A good horse makes it a pleasure. Your mount’s a good-looking animal.”

“His name’s Coronado,” I say. I scan the big bay that Tunstall is riding. It’s a magnificent beast. “I think your horse is the best I’ve ever seen.”

Tunstall smiles at the compliment. “His name’s Dalston, after the place I was born in London.

There are very few people who come close to Dalston in my affections."

"I don't name my horses," Bill says sullenly. He's been in a miserable mood all morning, very different from the happy-go-lucky companion on the trail yesterday. "Ain't never kept one long enough to need to."

I ignore Bill's comment. "Why are we taking the horses up to Lincoln to sell?" I ask Tunstall.

"Now that's a much more complicated question than you think. You are aware that McSween and I are setting up a trading and ranching business in opposition to the monopoly that Dolan holds in Lincoln?"

"I am," I reply. "Bill told me something of it."

"Then you will know that Dolan has not taken kindly to having opposition. He's trying everything to discourage us. He's hired Jesse Evans and his boys, a disreputable gang of cutthroats if I ever saw one, to threaten my men and me. Why, they even tried to provoke me into a gunfight in the main street of Lincoln, as if I was some hired gunman." Tunstall laughs and I join him. The image of this suave Englishman being drawn into a brutal street fight with some hired killer is just too unlikely.

"When he saw he couldn't drive us out with threats, Dolan resorted to the law, or what passes for it in this remote place where every judge is in Dolan's pocket."

"That snake William Brady too," Bill mutters under his breath.

"Who's William Brady?" I ask.

"Sheriff in Lincoln," Tunstall tells me. "Although the title gives him too much honor. He's little more than one of Dolan's hired men. Anyway, to get back to the horses, McSween was using the law to help us, so Dolan had one of their tame lawyers draw up a warrant against him, claiming he was in debt to them. It's nonsense, but it will take time to settle, which is what Dolan wants.

"According to the warrant, McSween's cattle are subject to seizure, but not these horses. I received word yesterday that Brady was coming out to the ranch to seize the cattle, so I thought it best to remove the horses today to avoid any unpleasantness over them. I think it also best if we are not at the ranch when Brady arrives. Some of my men"—Tunstall glances at Bill—"can be a trifle hotheaded under pressure."

"Turkey chase," one of the hands yells as five or six large birds explode from a nearby stand of trees. Immediately, three of the hands launch into a gallop after the animals, leaving only Brewer and a man called

Middleton with the horses. Bill wheels his horse and rides out to join the hunt.

"What about the horses?" I ask Tunstall.

"Don't worry about them. They're well trained. As long as Dick Brewer and Middleton stay ahead and I sit behind, they'll keep plodding along the trail until you boys come back with some excellent fat wild turkeys for the dinner pot. Off you go."

I hesitate, but Tunstall smiles and nods at the men who are careening wildly about the hillside after the panicked birds. I smile back. In less than a day, I have become very fond of my new boss. I'm going to enjoy working for him. His easygoing attitude and ready smile remind me of my father. I trot off after Bill.

I've almost reached the crest of a low rise, about half a mile from the trail, when I hear a shout behind me. I rein in Coronado and look back. Four men are riding along the trail toward Tunstall. Several others are following them, spread out along the valley. Brewer is riding toward us, calling and pointing at the pursuers. Bill has heard the shouts and arrives at my side.

"That's Jesse Evans," he says under his breath. "Looks like Billy Morton, Tom Hill and Frank Baker with him."

"Dolan and Riley's men. What are they doing here?"

"No good," Bill replies. He stands in his stirrups and shouts, "Mr. Tunstall. Get away from the horses. Come up here."

Tunstall seems unsure of what to do. Middleton is riding back toward him. "Come away, Mr. Tunstall," Middleton shouts as he swings his horse up the slope toward us. A shot rings out with startling clarity in the still morning air. I don't know who fired it or who it was aimed at, but it is followed in quick succession by three or four others.

Middleton spurs his horse on, shouting urgently back over has shoulder, "Come on, Mr. Tunstall. Those boys mean us harm."

Tunstall, still looking around uncertainly, slowly leaves the horses. Evans and the other three ignore us and ride toward Tunstall who stops after he has gone a few yards and turns back.

"No." I hear Bill say, under his breath.

Tunstall appears to be talking to the approaching men. He has dropped his reins and spreads his hands out wide, palms up to show he is not holding his gun. The four men slow to a trot, and Bill and I, joined now by Brewer and Middleton, watch the scene unfold. We are too far off to do anything.

Tunstall keeps talking, and the four men sit, spread apart, and appear to be listening. Maybe it's just some misunderstanding. Tunstall is waving up the trail at the horses, which are standing around grazing idly now that no one is urging them on. He's obviously explaining that these animals are not part of the warrant that Sheriff Brady has issued.

"Just give them the horses," Brewer says under his breath.

Without warning, one of the men raises his rifle and shoots Tunstall full in the chest. For a moment, the Englishman sits immobile, his hands still held out wide; then he slips sideways and falls to the ground. His bay horse skitters a few steps to one side, confused by the noise and the loss of its rider.

Tunstall is lying on his front, struggling to push himself up with his arms. A second of the attackers dismounts and walks calmly over to stand above Tunstall, who twists his head to look up. The effort seems too much, and he sags back down. In one swift motion, the standing man draws his pistol and fires one shot into the back of Tunstall's head. The body jerks and lies still.

Bill screams a string of foul curses, drags his Colt out of its holster and urges his horse forward. Brewer lunges forward and grabs his reins to hold him back. Bill turns to stare at Brewer. His eyes are cold. "Drop the reins, Dick," he says quietly, raising his pistol and pointing it at Brewer's head. "They murdered Tunstall in cold blood, and I aim to make them pay. I don't want to have to kill you as well."

Brewer holds his ground. "You can shoot me now, Bill, but all that'll mean is that we'll both be dead. Look."

We all turn our attention back to the valley. Several riders are arriving to join the original four. I count fourteen in total.

"We'll pay them back, Bill," Brewer says, "and I'll be right by your side when we do, but now's not the time."

Bill holds Brewer's eye for a long minute, then slowly lowers his gun. "John Tunstall was the only man that ever treated me like I was free-born and a man. Morton shot him first and Hill finished him off like he was a sick dog. I swear in front of all you boys that I will kill those two and everyone who helped them murder John Tunstall, or I will die trying."

"And we're all with you in that, Bill," Brewer says. He looks at each of us in turn. When his eyes meet mine, I, too, nod in agreement, although I'm uncertain what I'm agreeing to. The sudden violence in the valley has left an empty feeling in the pit of my stomach and the sensation that things are spinning out of control around me.

Below us, Hill pulls Tunstall's revolver out of its holster and fires two shots in the air. He then places the gun by the corpse's hand.

"What'd he do that for?" I ask.

"So he can say Tunstall fired back," Bill says bitterly. "Claim it were self-defence not murder."

Hill says something to Morton, who laughs. Then he calmly walks over to Tunstall's magnificent horse and shoots it between the eyes. The horse shudders, takes two steps back and collapses on the ground. Bill hisses a curse.

Evans is now pointing up the slope at us, and several men are forming up as if to charge us.

"Time we were gone," Brewer says. Bill hesitates, itching for a fight, to do something to revenge his friend. "Come on, Bill," Brewer encourages. "We can't do anything more here."

"You're dead men," Bill shouts down the hillside at Morton, Hill, Baker and Evans. Reluctantly, he turns his horse and we ride off into the trees. I wonder how things can change so abruptly. Even though I only knew him for less than twenty-four hours, John Tunstall was my friend. In minutes, I have gone from being a ranch hand to a witness to murder and a member of a gang that has sworn revenge. What worries me is that Tunstall's murder is a beginning not an end, and that I have no way of knowing what, where or when the real end will be.

The undertaker has done the best he can to prepare the body lying in the coffin balanced across two chairs in the dining room of Tunstall's house in Lincoln. However, there is a limit to his skill, and against the body's marble-white skin, the bullet's ragged exit hole in the forehead above the left eye looks black and evil. The face is also heavily scratched from encounters with heavy brush after it was loaded onto a burro and brought back to town.

"Every one of those rats who done this is still out there, free to live the high life and go where they want." Bill is pacing back and forth along the length of the room like some caged animal, desperate to break out and run riot. "We should get a gang together and have done with it," Bill continues without stopping his pacing. "Kill 'em all—Dolan, Evans, Morton, Baker, Hill."

"And what about Sheriff Brady?" Dick Brewer asks quietly.

"Him, too, if he stands in our way."

"And the judge, and the soldiers they'll send down from Fort Stanton?" Brewer continues. "And then we'll ride on up to Santa Fe and kill all the politicians and businessmen there, because they're the ones who are really behind all this?"

Bill grunts and falls silent.

"We all need to calm down," Brewer says. "It's only been four days since the murder. We'll bury John this afternoon and then attend to business. And we'll do it legal."

"Legal!" Bill stops and stares hard at the ranch foreman across the open coffin. "There weren't *nothing* legal about John's murder. Anyways, how we going to do anything legal when every lawman in the county's in Dolan's pocket?"

Bill, Brewer and I are in the room, paying our last respects to Tunstall and trying to decide what to do next. Everyone's been angry, but Bill's anger is different. It's wild enough, but there's a cold edge to it.

The night after we brought Tunstall's body back to town, everyone got roaring drunk, staggering around swearing hideous vengeance on Evan's gang. Bill never touched a drop of liquor. He just sat in the shadows, cleaning his Winchester and his Colt and staring blankly into the fireplace with a look that sent shivers down my spine.

"Not every lawman," Brewer goes on. "The Justice of the Peace, John Wilson, he's as straight as they come. People call him the Squire because of his fairness. He'll deputize us, and then we can go after Tunstall's killers."

"And hand them over to Sheriff Brady so they can be let off or allowed to escape?" Bill's voice is heavy with sarcasm.

"I don't know," Brewer admits, "but I do know we're not going rampaging around town, guns blazing. Once we've captured John's killers, we'll let McSween handle the legal side of it."

Bill is silent for a long time.

"All right," he says eventually. "We'll do it your way, for now." He turns on his heel and stalks out of the room. I look at Brewer. He appears tired and worried. I turn and follow Bill.

Bill's sitting on the edge of the stone horse trough behind the house. I walk over and join him. He's staring at the water in the trough and doesn't look up when I arrive, but he starts talking.

"I thought when I come to work here that I'd found the da that my real das never were. A chance to make something of my life. Work for Tunstall for a year or two, collect a grubstake and maybe try my hand at ranching. I even talked about going in with a couple of the boys here, and Tunstall said he would help us get going.

"There's still land to be had cheap over by the Arizona Territory border, nothing fancy, just enough to run a few cattle, too small to be of interest to the rustlers, and if we could keep the Apaches away for a few years, we reckoned we could build something."

"You still can," I say.

Bill laughs. "You're a good kid, and I might even have offered you a share, but you're naive. The big boys like Dolan'll never let the likes of me make a go of it. To them, I'm nothing but a no-good troublemaker, and perhaps they're right, maybe that's all I am."

"What do you mean?" I'm shocked and confused by Bill's negativity. Where's the cheerful companion I met on the trail a few days back?

Bill looks up from the trough. I expect his face to show sadness, but it doesn't. There's no emotion at all, and his eyes are cold and empty. It's as if he's talking about someone he doesn't know or care about.

"Trouble follows me. Even as a boy in Wichita and Silver City, I was always getting in trouble. Not for anything real bad, just high jinks, kid's stuff. Ma did the best she could, sent me to school to get some learning, taught me to dance at home, got in a Mexican woman to teach me Spanish. I even got jobs on ranches or in stores, but something always went wrong. Some dumb cowboy'd try to bully me 'cause I looked skinny and young. Or I'd find the storekeep cutting the flour with sawdust, and I'd fight back. Next thing I knew I'd be in jail. Once you're branded, don't matter what you do. Do the right thing, you still end up in jail, so what's the point in trying? If I'm going to jail for fighting off a bully, I might as well go for stealing a good horse.

"That Cahill fella I shot over in Camp Grant, it were self-defence all right. Brute would've broke my back if I hadn't. But it scared me just the same. That's why I come over here to make a new start. It's no small matter to kill a man."

Bill's voice has softened, and his gaze drifts thoughtfully over the trough. Then his shoulders stiffen and he stares back at me, his features hardened.

"Least, that's what I used to think. After I saw Morton shoot John in the chest and Hill finish him off with a shot to the head…killing them, or Baker and Evans, would mean no more to me now than stepping on a bug. Easiest thing in the world, and I aim to do it too."

"What about Brewer's plan to become deputies?" I ask, shocked at Bill's casual talk of murder.

"Oh, I'll go along with that, as far as I need to. I'll tell you one thing though. If I'm with the posse that takes any of those boys, they won't live more'n an hour after they're captured."

Bill stands and stalks back into the house, leaving me confused and worried.

It's nearly two weeks since we put John Tunstall in the ground, and I'm a deputy. So's Bill and Dick Brewer and about a dozen others. We don't have badges, but we've each got a piece of paper from "Squire" Wilson deputizing us. Brewer also has a warrant indicting Morton, Baker, Hill, Evans and several others who ride with them. We call ourselves Regulators, and based on a tip from William McCloskey, nine of us are trailing two of Jesse Evans's men now, through the hills east of Lincoln.

"I sure hope it's Morton and Baker," Bill says. He's riding beside me, and this is the first thing he's said since we set out at first light this morning. We heard yesterday that Evans and Hill are over at Tularosa, so it's unlikely to be them, and these four are the ones Bill holds most to blame for Tunstall's murder.

Over the past few days, Bill's been painfully quiet, responding to questions with grunts or single words. It's as if he's so single-mindedly focused on revenge that anything else is a distraction.

"McCloskey says Morton and Baker were headed down toward Mexico today. We've picked up the fresh trail of two riders heading that way. Why would he lie?"

"I don't trust McCloskey," Bill says sullenly. "He's friends with Morton and used to ride with Evans. Why would he sell out his friend?"

"Because he's a murderer," I say, but it sounds weak. If I'm honest, I don't trust McCloskey either. He has a narrow rat face and his eyes are never still, continually darting off to the side when he talks to you instead of meeting you confidently. "We're following someone. We'll be caught up with them soon, then we can see what's to be done."

At the front of our posse, Brewer holds up his hand and we rein in around him. Ahead the trail splits in two.

"Now," Brewer says casually, "if I were heading down to Mexico, I'd take the left trail, it's longer but it's easier and you can make better time. Seems, though, that our boys have taken the right trail through the canyon."

"Then why're we sitting here jawing?" Bill asks. "Let's get on after them."

Brewer gives Bill a long, hard look.

"We're not far behind these boys. I reckon, if we take the easier trail, we might well get to where the trails join once more before them. That way, all we have to do is sit and wait rather than panicking them into a gallop by coming up behind them on a narrow trail."

There's a murmur of agreement from the others.

"We should follow them on the right fork," McCloskey says. His voice sounds high-pitched and nervous. Several of us glance at him. "I mean, we've come all this way. We don't want to lose them by taking the wrong trail."

"I don't aim to lose them," Bill says. "Brewer makes sense. Let's get going." He pushes his horse forward and starts off down the left-hand fork.

"Bill sure is keen to catch these boys," someone comments as we get moving. McCloskey hangs back uncertainly but eventually follows on.

"I don't want no shooting unless they shoot first." Brewer is addressing everyone, but he's looking at Bill. We're scattered through some scrub trees on both sides of the trail about a half mile past where the two forks rejoin. "We'll take them in for trial."

Bill snorts derisively but says nothing. Tensions are mounting. Waiting in ambush is much harder than riding along the trail, and like Brewer, I'm nervous about what Bill will do when we catch Morton and Baker.

"Here they come," the whispered message is passed among us. We all shrink back farther in among the trees. Two men are riding slowly along the trail, frequently glancing back the way they have come. I don't know if it's Morton and Baker, but I sense Bill tense beside me.

As the riders draw level, Bill spurs his horse and bursts onto the trail in front of them. Both men immediately turn, but the other Regulators are emerging from the trees and there's no escape. One of the men is large and stockily built, the other is tall but skinny. Both are dressed in work clothes and covered with dust from the trail.

"Hello, Bill," the big man says. He appears calm, but his companion is terrified, blinking rapidly and looking around the armed men surrounding him. "What brings you out here?"

"You do, Billy Morton." Bill's voice is quiet, but he has everyone's attention. Several of the men have drawn their weapons, but Bill's Colt Thunderer is still in the holster at his waist. "You and your little sneak friend, Frank Baker."

"Why would that be?" Morton asks. The man's a murderer, but I can't help but admire his coolness.

"We seen you, Morton. Seen you shoot John Tunstall in the chest as he rode up to surrender to you. And we seen you too, Baker." The skinny man flinches as if physically struck when Bill shifts his gaze onto him.

"What d'you aim to do with us?" Morton asks.

"Take you in to stand trial for murder," Brewer says, pushing his way forward. "We're legal deputies, sworn in by Justice Wilson, and we've got legal warrants for your arrest. You as well, Frank."

"Well, now, here's an interesting situation." Morton is smirking confidently. "You boys are deputies sworn in by 'Squire' Wilson, and me and Frank are deputies sworn in by Sheriff Brady. Seems we'd be as likely to arrest you."

"Except there's nine of us and only two of you," Brewer points out.

"Well, now," Morton acknowledges, "you do have a point there. I reckon we'll just come along peacefully." He holds his hands out in front of him, wrists together.

Bill moves forward, reaching for the rope looped around his saddle horn. Everyone relaxes. Morton is smiling, and the tension is draining out of the situation. I watch Bill, but not the left hand that is lifting the rope. I watch Bill's right hand, and that's why I see what the others don't. His hand is edging toward his gun.

A sick feeling knots my stomach. I urge Coronado forward and yell, "Bill! No!" I'm too slow. With a movement as fast and smooth as a snake striking, Bill slides his gun out of its holster, points it at Morton's head and fires.

The big man has an instant of looking surprised, as the .41 caliber bullet smashes into his temple, tears through his brain and explodes out the back of his head in a spray of blood.

Everything happens in slow motion. Heads turn to watch Morton slide out of the saddle onto the ground. Frank Baker's horse shies in fear as Bill swings his Colt around toward its rider. I grab my friend's arm.

Bill's second shot flies wildly past the terrified Baker. Then I have the gun, and Brewer has positioned himself between Bill and Baker. "That's enough," he says. Bill doesn't struggle for his gun but sits calmly in the saddle, staring at Frank Baker over Brewer's shoulder.

"Don't let him shoot me," Baker pleads.

"No one's going to get shot," Brewer says.

"You're a dead man still breathing," Bill says in an emotionless voice that sends chills through everyone who hears it.

"Oh, God," Baker whimpers. He looks as if he's about to fall off his horse. "Don't let him kill me. I don't want to die." He reaches forward and tugs at Brewer's sleeve. "I know something. You protect me and I'll tell you."

Brewer turns to face Baker.

"You tell me or I'll shoot you myself."

"Okay. Okay. Listen. This were a trap. You were meant to follow us into the canyon. There's an ambush there." The words are spilling out of Baker like a waterfall with no space between them and barely time for breath. "The others aimed to catch you where the trail narrows."

I hear movement behind me, but my attention is completely on Baker's frantic tale.

"How did they know we would be following you?" Brewer asks.

I suddenly realize what's going on. McCloskey set us up. Before I can say anything, I'm startled by another gunshot. Baker cartwheels backward off his horse. I turn, but already McCloskey has forced his horse past the surrounding men and is riding hard away from us. Without thinking, I raise Bill's Colt and fire. The double action is incredible. All I have to do is keep pulling the trigger. Before I realize it, I've fired four shots and the hammer clicks on an empty chamber.

Several other men are firing at McCloskey now and he slows. He makes a weak attempt to turn and fire back, but gives up and slumps forward across his horse's neck. Two men ride toward him.

"Smooth action." I turn to see Bill looking at me. Despite all the violence, he's still sitting relaxed in his saddle. He holds out his hand. "Beats your old gun, don't it?"

I pass the empty Colt over to Bill, who slips it back into his holster. "Looks like we got one each, Jim."

"No," I say. "You shot Morton in cold blood. I shot a fugitive trying to escape."

"That right? Well, whatever the details, I reckon one's as dead as the other now." Bill's knowing smile makes me feel intensely uncomfortable.

I dismount angrily and push past Bill's horse to help Brewer lift Frank Baker's body onto his horse. I can convince myself that I shot in the heat of the moment, but I can't escape the fact that I've killed another man. What am I turning into?

7

"This is how it'll go down." We're well on the way back to town, the three dead men strapped across their horses. We collected the bodies as quickly as we could and left before anyone who could have heard the shooting showed up. Now we are gathered around Brewer. "We arrested Morton and Baker and were bringing them in. Morton shot McCloskey and we shot him and Baker while attempting to escape."

We all nod agreement. The story will work, as long as no one looks too closely at the wounds or asks too many questions. The group breaks up and we continue on our way. I drop to the back and ride alone, deep in thought.

I feel as if I'm losing control of my life since I met Bill and came to Lincoln County. Some very strange things happened last year while I was looking for my father, and I did some things I'm not too proud of, but I was always in control. Not that I could always influence events, but what I could do was always up to me. I had a goal, to get to Casas Grandes and find out what happened to my father, and I kept at it until my task was complete. I didn't find the answers I expected, but I did find answers.

Up here the situation is different. Other than the vague idea of getting work, I wasn't pursuing a goal when I came here. I thought I had landed on my feet when I met Bill and began work for Tunstall, but Tunstall's dead and Bill is not what he seemed. I was wracked by guilt after I killed the kid in the pork-pie hat, but death doesn't seem to bother Bill, even when he causes it. Am I becoming more like him?

"Jim, isn't it?" I'm brought out of my reverie by Brewer dropping back and falling in beside me.

"Yes," I answer, "Jim Doolen."

"Well, Jim," Brewer asks, "you comfortable with what happened back there?"

I'm not sure what Brewer's getting at, but he seems like a decent man. It's him that's tried all though this to get things done the proper, legal, way.

"No," I answer honestly. "Bill was wrong to shoot Morton like that. I can understand that he wants revenge on Tunstall's killers. And Morton and Baker, and probably McCloskey, too, deserved to pay for what they did, but shooting him like that without any trial was wrong."

"I agree with what you say," Brewer says. "Bill can be charming and good company, but since Tunstall's murder I've seen a different side to him, a cold calculating side that thinks nothing of shooting a man in the head without warning. You can't control a man like that. He's not bound by the same rules as the rest of us."

I nod agreement. Bill's like two men living in the same body, a fun-loving boy and a hard-eyed killer.

"What're your plans?"

"I don't know," I say. "I haven't thought much about it with all that's been going on."

"I hope you'll stay on with us. McSween plans to continue with the ranch and the store, and we need good men like you."

I'm flattered that Brewer values me, but I have a question. "What about Bill?"

"Unfortunately, as long and Dolan's hiring men like Jesse Evans and his gang, we also need men like Bill.

He'll calm down now that Morton and Baker are dead, and I can keep him in line. Will you stay on?"

"I will," I reply. After all, I don't have anything else to do. I just hope Brewer is right about being able to keep Bill under control.

8

The three weeks after the killings pass uneventfully. I don't think Sheriff Brady and the others in Lincoln believed our story about how Morton, Baker and McCloskey died, but I don't think they would have believed any story we told. And, in any case, they have little choice. We were legal deputies exercising a warrant and we all tell the same version of events. I don't feel comfortable with the lies, but I bury my uneasiness in memories of how Morton, Hill, Evans and Baker executed Tunstall.

Two days after we get back to town, we hear that Hill and Evans have been shot while stealing sheep down by Tularosa. Hill's dead, and Evans is so badly wounded that he's taken refuge in Fort Stanton. Three of the four men who are most directly responsible for Tunstall's death are now dead and the fourth is unreachable in army custody. Perhaps that will satisfy Bill. Perhaps, but somehow I doubt it.

Mostly, I work on McSween's ranch and in the hills round about. And Coronado and I enjoy learning the ins and outs of running his three hundred and fifty head of cattle. I don't see much of Bill and the other Regulators. Sometimes they work on the ranch, but often they disappear for a few days. On one occasion, a Regulator returns from one of these expeditions with a bullet that needs to be dug out of his shoulder or his leg. I know they're out hunting the boys who ride with Evans and that an almost continual running battle is happening in the hills around Lincoln, but I try to ignore it.

On the morning of the last day of March, Brewer approaches me. "Got a job for you, Jim," he says. "I want you to load the wagon up with the prime sides of beef we butchered last night and get them on up to Fort Stanton. You'll have to stop in Lincoln and pick up some dry goods from the store." He hands me a piece of paper with a scrawled list on it. "Don't hang around. See if you can get to Stanton tonight or first thing tomorrow morning. We don't want the meat going off and spoiling the officers' dinner."

"No problem," I say.

"You ain't done then," Brewer continues. "After you've unloaded, I want you to swing down to La Luz and pick up a couple of horses the army wants. They're being held at the livery stable there. The officer at Fort Stanton'll give you the bill of sale. Pick the horses up and deliver them back to Fort Stanton, and the officer'll pay you for the dry goods and the horses then. Round trip should take no more'n a week, so wait at the fort and me and some of the boys'll come up April sixth or seventh to escort you and the money back."

"No problem," I repeat. "Will you look after Coronado while I'm gone?"

"I'll do that," Brewer replies. "He'll be waiting for you when you return."

I'm looking forward to the trip. It'll be a slow, bumpy ride in the unsprung cart drawn by two mules, but I'll be on my own and I enjoy that. It'll also get me away from Bill and the Regulators for a while.

Bill's at the ranch, and he helps me load the meat.

"Go as quick as you can, Jim," he says when I'm ready to set off. "See if you can make Fort Stanton tonight."

"It'll be dark for sure before I get there," I say. "What's the hurry? Brewer says tomorrow first thing is all right."

"I got my reasons." Anger flashes in Bill's eyes. "Don't listen to Brewer, just do what I say."

"Okay," I agree, knowing from experience that it doesn't pay to argue with Bill when his mood swings like this. "I'll try to make Fort Stanton tonight."

Bill nods and his angry expression turns to a smile.

"Good lad. Things'll be different when you get back." He slaps the rump of one of the mules and the wagon jerks forward. I concentrate on persuading the mules to pass through the ranch gate and keep to the trail, wondering what Bill means by things being different.

I set off in good time, but the going is slow and I'm held up when one of the mules throws a shoe. By the time I reach town and load the supplies, the sun is touching the western hills and thunderclouds are gathering to the north. Whatever Bill says, I'm not driving the nine miles out to the fort in the dark and a thunderstorm. I decide to bed down in the back room of Tunstall's store and set off first thing in the morning.

I have a comfortable night on a pile of blankets and flour sacks and am up at first light. I go out back into the corral to wash off the sleep in the horse trough before setting off on the trail. As I stand up, shaking the cold water off my face and out of my hair, I notice several men crouching behind the low adobe wall that runs out from the corner of the store. As I watch, a figure stands up and I recognize Bill. Curious, I cross the corral. The wall is only about four feet high, but several holes have been dug through the soft bricks.

Bill and five Regulators are sitting in the dirt, their horses hitched to the rail nearby. Each man has a rifle beside him. I have a bad feeling, but before I can retreat, Bill sees me. I expect anger that I am still in town but, as always, Bill's mood is unpredictable. "Jim," he says cheerfully, "you come to join our little prank for April Fool's Day?"

"What prank?" I ask.

Behind Bill a Regulator hisses, "He's coming." Immediately, all the men grab their rifles and crouch down by the holes in the wall.

I turn and look back down the street. Sheriff Brady and four of his deputies are coming along. The only ones I recognize are George Hindman and Bob Beckwith. The group is relaxed, sauntering out in the open, talking casually. I duck down beside Bill. "What's going on?"

"We got tired of riding all over them hills chasing shadows," he says, never taking his eye from the hole in the wall in front of him. "Don't make too much sense, far as I can see, so me and some of the fellas decided to get to the root of the problem."

"What do you mean?" I ask, although I'm beginning to suspect I know.

"Brady's the law hereabouts. Without him, we stand a chance."

"You're planning to kill him." I begin to stand up, with some vague idea of shouting a warning, but Bill is suddenly looking at me, his Colt in his hand. "You stay right where you are, young Jim Doolen. If you try to interfere, I swear to God I'll put a bullet through your head as easy as I did Morton's."

I haven't the slightest doubt that Bill will do exactly that if he feels the need. I slump down against the wall, being careful to keep my hands in sight and well clear of my holster. Bill returns his attention to the hole in the wall but keeps his revolver pointed in my direction.

"Where's Brewer?" I ask. "Does he know you're doing this?"

"Dick Brewer's a good man," Bill says out of the side of his mouth, "but he don't ride the hills with us. He ain't seen what Evans and his boys can do.

"You didn't come with us to collect Tunstall's body, but Evans had laid it out with John's overcoat as a pillow and his blanket covering him, like he was sleeping under the stars and not lying there with a hole through his head."

"Doesn't that show some respect for the body?" I ask, even though I doubt Evans and the others are the sort to care about respect.

"They done it for a joke," Bill says bitterly. "You see, they'd done the same to his favorite horse, pillowed its head as if it were sleeping beside John." Bill glances at me and smiles when he sees the look of shock on my face. "You saw what Morton, Evans and the others were capable of," he continues, turning his gaze back to the street. "Now, I don't blame them for that, but as long as they've got the law on their side, they've got an unfair advantage and they'll always do just as they please."

"Killing Brady's not going to solve that," I say.

"That it won't," Bill agrees, "but it's a start. Maybe the next sheriff won't be so keen to do what Dolan tells him. Now you just sit there quiet until this's over."

I do as I'm told. What choice to I have? When have I ever had choices since I came to this godforsaken place? I sag back against the wall, feeling the rough adobe bricks through my shirt. The sun has risen and warms my face. It's going to be a beautiful day.

A ragged volley of shots rings out in the still air. I watch Bill, his Colt now on the ground beside him, work the lever on his Winchester, sending the brass cartridges spinning away in the sunlight.

Eventually, the shooting stops and several Regulators stand up to look over the top of the wall. I join them. Brady is on his knees in the middle of the street, a cloud of dirty gray smoke from the gunfire drifting by him. He's still alive but only just. The front of his shirt is torn in three or four places and already soaked in blood. His left arm hangs twisted and useless by his side, and his right cheek is torn away and bleeding. He's swaying from side to side, his eyes drifting aimlessly around, and he's groaning, "Oh, Lord, I'm dead," over and over. Hindman is also hit and lying on the street, attempting to crawl away. The others have taken cover across the street.

Despite his wounds, Brady is struggling to stand. Calmly, Bill works the lever of his Winchester, ejecting the empty cartridge and loading a fresh one. In one smooth motion he aims and fires. The bullet catches Brady full in the chest. He falls backward and lies still.

Bob Beckwith runs out into the open and attempts to haul Hindman to safety. Two more shots ring out and Hindman goes limp. Beckwith retreats to cover.

"We got him," Bill yells exultantly. He drops his Winchester, grabs his pistol and vaults nimbly over the wall. He's followed by one of the Regulators, a man called Jim French. The pair stroll casually across the street toward Brady. Bill is smiling. He leans over Brady's body and says something. I can't hear and don't know if he's talking to the dead man or French.

Beckwith stands up and aims his rifle at Bill. The bullet tears a gouge in Bill's thigh and nicks French's calf. Both men shout in anger and a volley of shots is unleashed from the wall, but Beckwith has ducked back down.

Cursing and clutching his thigh, Bill hobbles back to the wall. French joins him. "Let me see the wound, Bill," he says.

Bill waves him away. "It's only a flesh wound. Nothing but a graze. Let's get out of here."

The Regulators collect their weapons and move to where their horses are tethered. Bill looks at me.

"You didn't give Brady a chance," I say.

"Same chance he'd have given me," he says. "And the next time I see Beckwith, I'll not give him a chance neither. This is how this war's playing out, Jim. There's no rules, and the winner'll be the last one standing."

"This is no better than the gang was in New York that you told me your dad was involved in. Didn't your mother move you away so the same thing wouldn't happen to you?"

Bill frowns, and for a moment I wonder if he's going to shoot me too. Instead he smiles—a cold, mirthless expression.

"I thought you'd care more about getting even with Tunstall's murderers."

"I do care," I say, "but this has gone way past that. Tunstall's dead. The men who killed him are dead. This is just fighting and killing for the sake of it, and I want no part of that."

"Suit yourself." Bill begins to hobble toward the horses, but he stops and turns back to me. "Just remember, Jim, in a war you have to take sides. If you don't, you become the enemy of both."

I stand and watch Bill cross the corral, struggle into the saddle and lead the Regulators out of town. As the hoofbeats die away, the only sound left is the barking of the town dogs. It seems I'm destined to be caught in the middle of this war, regardless of whether I take sides or not. Maybe I should just ride away and lead the solitary life I did before. At least then I could make my own decisions. First, though, I have to finish my job for Brewer.

Feeling miserable, I cross the street to get the wagon ready for the journey to Fort Stanton and La Luz. Brady is lying on his side in a large pool of blood. Already a swarm of flies is gathering in the warming air. Several people have gathered around Brady and Hindman. They watch me warily as I pass, but I ignore them. I want nothing to do with either side. All I want right now is to get on the trail and be alone and work out how to get back control of my life.

"**I**'ve brought the sides of beef and dry goods from the McSween place," I tell a pair of guards standing casually by the road where it enters the buildings of Fort Stanton. They're Buffalo Soldiers and remind me of the column I met on the trail down to Casas Grandes.

"Wait here," one of the men orders before he heads off to find an officer.

The other guard looks into the wagon disinterestedly and then resumes his place beside the road. I take the opportunity to look around.

Apart from the neat regimented rows of white tents covering the flat valley bottom, Fort Stanton does not look very military. In fact, it looks like a more prosperous, well-established community than Lincoln.

There are some thirty stone and wooden buildings scattered among the trees at the foot of the rolling hills beside the river. The main ones are set in a vast square around an open parade ground. Several of the buildings are two or three stories high. Many are surrounded by wide verandas and all are immaculately maintained and painted. I can see a smithy, stables, the outdoor ovens of a bakery and a hospital. A long barrack building runs down one side of the parade square, and a squad of soldiers is practicing drill at the foot of a tall flagpole. The military feel of the scene is weakened by five Apache women carrying large laundry baskets up from the river.

Farther up the valley, I can see a collection of wickiups, outside of which several Apache men and women sit around fires. I assume they are awaiting escort down to the reservation in Tularosa Canyon.

Eventually I spot the soldier returning.

"Lieutenant Fowler says to take the wagon over to the store room." He points to a low building across the open space. "He'll delegate some men to unload it. The Lieutenant requests that you join him in the officers' quarters yonder." Once more he points, this time at a fine two-story stone building fronted by a wide-pillared veranda. The soldier loses interest in me and rejoins his comrade.

I urge the mules into movement and head toward the store. I'm pretty sure that Fowler was the name of the young officer I met on the way to Casas Grandes last year, and there are unlikely to be two lieutenants with the same name in such a small area. I wonder what it'll be like to meet him again. He was helpful to me, but his characterization of the Apaches as savages had jarred with my experience in meeting Wellington and Nah-kee-tats-an.

I ask a soldier outside the officers' quarters where to go and am directed to a door farther down the veranda. I knock and a familiar voice bids me enter.

Lieutenant Fowler looks cleaner but otherwise much the same as when we last met. He looks up from a crude desk as I enter, and his brow furrows in puzzlement. "Do I know you?" he asks.

"You do," I say with a smile. "I'm Jim Doolen. We met on the trail south of Tucson last December. You were bringing the bodies of two men back to Fort Bowie."

"Yes. Yes," Fowler says, standing and extending his hand. I shake it, and he ushers me to a chair. "You were headed for Casas Grandes, I recall. Did you make it there without mishap?"

"I did."

"So what brings you up here to this troubled part of the world?"

"I came here looking for work."

"And found some, it seems. You're working for McSween?"

"Yes. I was hired by John Tunstall, the day before he was murdered."

"Bad business that, and getting worse from what I understand."

"It is," I agree. "Sheriff Brady was shot and killed this very morning in the main street of Lincoln."

"In the main street, you say. In broad daylight?"

"Just after dawn," I say. "One of his deputies was killed with him."

"It's a disgrace," Fowler reflects. "There's no law. If it were up to me, I'd ride in there with my company and arrest the lot, Dolan, Evans and the Regulators. It's not as if we don't have enough trouble with the Apaches coming and going off the reservation as they please and causing havoc over in Texas."

"Can't the army do anything?"

"It seems not. Colonel Dudley claims he has orders not to interfere in civilian matters. And that may be true, but he's awful ready to entertain Dolan to dinner in the mess, and I received quite the talking-to for ordering this one wagonload you've brought from McSween.

"But listen to me croak on like a bitter old man." Fowler reaches into a drawer in his desk and pulls out a sheet of paper. "This is the bill of sale for the horses you're to bring back from La Luz. They're being held at the livery stable there."

"Thank you," I say, taking the paper and folding it.

"And you'll stay with us tonight and dine as my guest in the mess," Fowler says. It's not a question. "A good night's sleep before a journey is a splendid start."

I agree readily. I enjoy Fowler's company, and the Fort seems an island of sanity in the chaos of the past few weeks. I excuse myself and go to tend to the mules and organize my bedroll.

"Why are you up here? When I met you in December, you and your company were headed for Fort Bowie." Lieutenant Fowler and I are standing on the veranda of the officers' mess. Dinner is over and Fowler has come out here to enjoy the cool evening air. He's smoking a long strong-smelling cheroot with obvious relish.

A half moon is hanging silver and bright above the trees.

"That was just a stop on a long patrol," he says. "Regimental headquarters for the Tenth Cavalry's at Fort Concho in Texas, but troops are spread all over the west, wherever there's a need, I reckon. B Troop's been here with units of the Ninth since last fall and will be for a time yet, I suspect. But it's not too bad. At least the fort's relatively civilized, much better than some sad collections of adobe and sticks that I've been quartered in."

"Why are your men called Buffalo Soldiers?" I voice a question that I've wondered about for a while.

"Number of stories about that." Fowler takes a long drag on his cheroot and watches the smoke drift into the evening air as he exhales. "Common one is that black soldiers' curly hair reminds the Apaches of the hair of a buffalo, but I heard one that makes more sense.

"Back in '67 when the Tenth was a new regiment, a Private Randall was assigned to look after a couple of greenhorn civilian hunters. They had the bad luck to run into a band of about seventy Cheyenne warriors. The hunters panicked and were picked off easily, and Randall's horse was shot from under him, but the trooper took cover in a washout under the railroad tracks they'd been following. He only had a pistol, but he held off the Cheyenne until help arrived.

"Story goes that there were more than a dozen dead warriors round the washout and that Randall had a gunshot wound in his shoulder and eleven lance wounds. The Cheyenne said that there was a new kind of warrior in the land, one that never gave up and fought like a cornered wild buffalo, and the name stuck."

"That's a good story," I say.

"And it might even be true," Fowler says with a smile. "These boys of mine fight like demons when they've a mind to. If you ever get the chance, get talking to Sergeant Rawlins. He was there at the very beginning. He fought with Shaw and the Fifty-fourth Massachusetts at Fort Wagner in '63. He can tell some stories."

"Were you in the Civil War?" I ask, hoping to encourage a story from Fowler.

"Naw, too young," he replies. "It's my lot to ride forever back and forth over this empty land collecting dust and scalped bodies. Mind you, I was lucky once."

"How so?" I ask when Fowler falls silent.

"I graduated from West Point in '76. I requested an assignment to the Seventh Cavalry. My brother, Miles, was serving in C Company. My request was approved, but fortunately I didn't reach them in time and was reassigned to the Tenth."

Lieutenant Fowler falls silent again. I'm confused about how this makes him lucky.

"Why didn't you join your brother in the Seventh?"

My companion turns to face me and smiles sadly in the flickering light of the hanging lantern. "C Company was wiped out with Custer at the Little Big Horn River."

"Your brother?"

Fowler nods and turns back to stare across the compound. Of all the stories I've collected over the past few months, Fowler's is the shortest, but it affects me deeply. I remember reading the newspaper accounts of Custer's men on that bare hillside in Montana Territory, knowing that they were going to die as overwhelming numbers of Sitting Bull's and Crazy Horse's warriors swarmed up from the valley to engulf them. Many a night I had lain awake wondering what I would do: fight to the last even though I knew it to be hopeless, beg for mercy, try to run in some futile attempt to escape? I had no way of knowing, but the horror of being one of those doomed men out on the bare prairie that afternoon as they watched their deaths approach sent shivers through me. And Lieutenant Fowler's brother had been one of them.

"Well," Fowler says at length, dropping the stub of his cheroot and grinding it beneath his boot heel, "nothing to be done. But listen." His voice perks up and he turns to me. "I would ask a favor of you."

"Ask away," I say.

"On your way back from La Luz, could you travel by Tularosa Canyon and try to determine what the mood is like on the reservation? The Mescaleros have been less trouble of late than some of the bands up at San Carlos, but I've been hearing tales of some young warriors slipping away to join the fighters in the hills. Frederick Godfroy's the agent there at Blazer's Mill and he'll give you a report to bring back. I also hear that Godfroy's wife Clara will cook you a dinner you'll remember for many months."

"I'd be glad to," I say. I sense that Fowler is about to bid me good night, but there's something I need to ask him before that. "When I met you on the trail, you readily dismissed the Apaches as savages. Now you seem almost respectful."

"Do I?" Fowler asks thoughtfully. "Perhaps I do. Certainly I have learned a lot since coming here. After Miles's death at the Little Big Horn, I felt a lot of hate and just wanted to come out here and kill as many Indians as I could, but it's not as simple as that, is it?"

I shake my head.

"Those two dead men I was bringing in when we met were road agents. Several folk at Fort Bowie recognized them as having caused considerable trouble recently on the surrounding trails. Worse than that, they were scalp hunters. I was told stories of days, not so long ago, when Indians—men, women and children—were hunted down and slaughtered like wild animals just for the value of their hair. Add to that this dirty little war that's going on in Lincoln County, and all the good men it's killing over a few sacks of flour, some sides of beef and a few dollars profit, and I got to wondering exactly who the savages are hereabouts."

I decide it's best not to mention my connection either to the scalp hunters or the Regulators. "I've met a couple of fine Apaches myself," I say.

Fowler looks at me with interest. "I suspect you have an interesting tale to tell, Jim Doolen. Perhaps when you return I shall have a chance to sit and listen. But for now I am going to turn in. I wish you a good journey until we meet again."

"Thank you." Fowler strolls down along the veranda, and I descend the steps and head across to the livery stable where I'll bed down for the night. I'm glad to have met Lieutenant Fowler once more. I hope he won't turn out to be as unreliable as Bill Bonney or as short-lived as John Tunstall. Perhaps if Brewer and Fowler get to talking, there might even be a way to end this bloodshed. At least it's a hope.

10

La Luz is a dirt-poor collection of adobe buildings scattered around the original Presidio Square. It nestles among the willows that line the banks of a dry riverbed and is overshadowed by the long shelves of rock that form the mountains I have just worked my way through. Most of the population are Mexican; Hispanics, they're called hereabouts. They remind me of my time last year at Esqueda and Casas Grandes.

When I arrive, there is some kind of fiesta going on, and the Presidio Square is decorated with colored paper and candles. A crude band is scratching and wheezing out a rough tune. A few of the locals, dressed in whatever colorful finery they possess, are either dancing

75

or sitting at tables, drinking from unmarked bottles and eating steaming plates of dark stew and tortillas.

I decide to join them. It's been a long journey. The horses I've come to collect can wait until tomorrow. I need some company and jollity after my time alone thinking about all the death I've seen of late.

I park the wagon at the livery stable, settle and feed the mules and stroll over to the square. I sit down and order a plate of stew and a bottle of the mescal everyone seems to be drinking. There are no other choices.

The stew is rich and spicy, and I wolf it and the accompanying plate of beans and tortillas down. Even the fiery mescal doesn't taste as harsh as the drink I remember Santiago giving me in Esqueda, if I sip it slowly.

I'm halfway through my food when an old man wanders toward me. He's bent over with age and walks with a pronounced limp. His dark wrinkled skin is dramatically set off by a mane of snow-white hair and he asks if he can join me.

"*Me puedo sentar con usted, señor?*" I wave to a chair, gesture at the bottle and ask if he speaks English.

The man sits down and pours himself a generous measure of the mescal. He drinks it down in one go.

"*Sí*, I do speak your language. I learned in Texas, and here this is an Americano world and it is necessary to speak the language."

"Texas is American too," I point out.

The old man smiles, showing a mouthful of surprisingly white teeth.

"Not always so. When I was born there, it was Mexico. Before the Americanos stole it."

"Stole it? The people who lived there had a revolution and became independent," I say indignantly. I've read several dime novels about the Alamo. How Davy Crocket and two hundred brave men held off the army of the cruel General Santa Anna for thirteen days before they were overwhelmed and killed.

Davy Crockett was one of my childhood heroes, fighting to the last and finally falling beneath a forest of bayonets, surrounded by the dozens of enemy soldiers he had killed. I spent many hours hunting squirrels in the woods around Yale, pretending I was fighting beside Crockett and yelling, "Remember the Alamo" every time one of the small animals dropped off a tree branch. What right did this ignorant old man have to attack my heroes?

The old man shakes with laughter.

"You Americanos and your stories. You do not listen. You just believe the first thing you hear that fits with what you wish to believe."

"I'm Canadian," I say crossly. My companion shrugs as if my distinction makes no difference to him. Without asking, he pours himself another drink. "Davy Crockett was a brave man," I add defensively.

"How do you know what happened to this *brave* man inside the walls of the mission at San Antonio de Bexar? Were you there?"

"No, I wasn't there. I read about it."

"And the man who wrote the book you read, was he there at the Alamo?"

"Of course not," I reply angrily. "No one survived the Alamo."

"No one?"

"I think the women and children were spared, but all the fighters were killed in the battle." I'm becoming confused about why this old man keeps harping on about this.

"All the Americanos."

"Yes, but…" I stutter to a stop as I realize what he means.

"Rather than reading books by men who sit in New York and make things up to sell for a dime each, would it not be better to ask one who was there?" The old man is grinning from ear to ear as he fills his glass once more.

"Of course," I say hesitantly, embarrassed at being caught out in my one-sided assumptions. "But how would I do that?"

"Ask away." The old man spreads his arms wide in invitation.

It takes me a minute to grasp what he means. "You!" He nods. "You were there?"

"That is how I acquired my limp," he says and slaps his thigh. "I was a boy, no older than you are now. A drummer in General Antonio Lopez de Santa Anna's army. Our motto was, 'Never one step backward.'"

Is the old man telling the truth? I have no reason to doubt him. If so, he has a story to tell. I look at him with new eyes. Maybe this man saw Davy Crockett or Jim Bowie.

"You say you want to know, and yet when you get the chance, you sit with your mouth open like a fish stranded on the riverbank."

I snap my mouth closed.

"What was it like?" I ask weakly.

"It was like war," he says. "It was dirty and chaotic. We were frightened and we were brave all at once.

There was dust and blood and noise and death, but do you not wish to know about your hero, Crockett?"

"Yes, and Bowie," I add hastily.

"Bowie I did not see," my companion says. My heart leaps because this implies that he did see Davy Crockett. "You understand everything happened very fast. It was all over in less than half an hour, although it seemed like a lifetime to us. I was in the third attack, the one that swarmed over the north wall. Those inside turned their cannon on us. The guns were filled with anything they could find—door hinges, rocks, pieces of horseshoes. They caused some hideous wounds and gave me my limp. I was hit in the leg by some Texian's heavy belt buckle. It broke the bone, and I played no further part in the fight but sat against the wall and watched the killing.

"The cannons didn't stop us. There was no time to reload, and our blood was up. My comrades killed all the Texians at the guns and anyone they found in the compound.

"I did not see Bowie, but I heard after he was found sick in a cot in a room by the wall, not far from where I sat. He shot the first man through the door, but the others bayoneted him as he lay there. He was a brave man. Sick as he was, he never tried to surrender. Not that it would have made any difference."

The old man falls silent. As he has talked, his gaze has moved away from me and his eyes focus more and more on the far distance, as if, behind me, he can see the drama of the Alamo being re-enacted. He is massaging his leg absently. I reach over, lift the half-empty bottle and refill his glass.

"*Gracias*," he says, his eyes coming back to life. "But you wish to know of Crockett. Him I saw. After we had taken the guns and the compound was secure, we had to fight through the rooms in the old mission. Four or five men would fire their muskets through the door and then rush in with bayonets and finish the job. It was hard, brutal work, and I am not sorry that my wound forced me to miss it.

"Everyone found in the mission was killed, except, as you say, for some women and children. We were not savages. We were ordered to kill them all. Santa Anna said the rebels were pirates, trying to steal land from Mexico, and that the only reward for piracy was death. One of our officers did not obey the order and took seven men prisoner. He brought them out into the compound in front of where I sat. They were a miserable collection of humanity—filthy, blood-covered and cowed. Several were wounded, one so badly he could not stand. Crockett was among those who surrendered.

He stood out from the rest, being taller and the only one who looked about and met the eyes of his captors. He even spoke at one point, suggesting that he be released to travel to the rest of the Texian army and negotiate a truce.

"When Santa Anna discovered that these men had been spared, he was furious and ordered them executed. We stood them against a wall, but the soldiers refused to shoot. The fight was done, we wished no more killing, but Santa Anna ordered his guard to do the work with sabers. I turned away, but I saw the bodies later. They were much cut about the head and arms. Only the man too badly wounded to stand had been shot where he lay on the ground."

"You're lying," I say, loudly enough for people nearby to stare. "Davy Crockett didn't surrender. He died fighting. He would never have asked to be spared."

The old man shrugs.

"That is your story. Believe it if you wish. I tell only what I saw with my own eyes. Remember, heroes and villains are what we make them. All are human."

The Mexican falls silent and I think about what he has told me. I don't want to believe him, but why not? I believed the stories that Wellington, Santiago and Ed told me, however unbelievable they seemed at the time.

The difference was, then I was seeking answers and hungrily absorbed anything that might help me find those answers. The story I was hearing now conflicted with something I already believed.

"You have come down from Lincoln?" The man interrupts my reverie.

"Yes. I'm collecting some horses to take back to Fort Stanton."

"You have your own war," the old man says slyly, "and heroes as well."

I think of Tunstall, taking on the corrupt Dolan syndicate. Maybe even Brewer, trying to continue the fight and hold the Regulators in check.

"I suppose we do."

"I have heard that the corrupt Sheriff Brady is dead."

"Yes, two days ago in Lincoln. He was shot in the main street from ambush."

"By El Chivato?"

"El Chivato?"

"The one you call Kid Antrim."

It takes me a moment to realize who he means. Is there an end to the number of names Bill goes by?

"Yes, it was Bill who shot him, although others were there."

The old man nods approvingly.

"There is a hero."

"Bill?"

"*Sí*, the one you call Bill. He is here often for our fiestas." The man looks around as if he expects to see Bill at the next table. "He is a fine dancer and a good singer." The man winks broadly. "He is a great favorite with the young *señoritas*." I suppose I must look puzzled, because he adds, "He is not a hero to you?"

"He's charming and friendly," I say, "but I've seen him shoot a man in the head in cold blood."

My companion smiles and takes another drink. "And this man did not deserve to die?"

"He was a murderer, but that's not the point."

"No? Murderers should, perhaps, be hanged by a sheriff and a judge with all the proper paperwork filled out?"

"Yes," I agree, but I hesitate.

"What if the sheriff is also a murderer, and the judge works for the same men who hired the killer?"

"I don't know," I say in confusion. "Things should be done legally."

"In a perfect world, yes, but the world is not perfect, especially in a war, and you are in a war, just as surely as I was in 1836 at the Alamo. Dolan is nothing, *nada*.

He is only a pawn of the political men in Santa Fe. He does what he is told. Do you see that man over there?" I follow the wave of the arm and see a young man talking with a dark-haired girl in a bright, flowing dress.

"Two years past, his brother, Miguel, owned a small ranch over in Tularosa Canyon near Blazer's Mill. He worked hard, struggling to run a ranch and raise a young family. He bought feed for his cattle on credit from Dolan and signed a promissory note to pay for it in three weeks. Two weeks later Jesse Evans and some others arrived at the ranch claiming that the bill was due. Miguel argued, but it was no good. Evans took his horse in payment, even though it was worth much more than the debt.

"After dark that night, Miguel tracked Evans and the others on foot, found their camp and tried to take his horse back. He was seen and captured, and at first light the next morning, Miguel's wife woke to find her husband's body propped against the back porch of the house. He had been beaten severely and shot five times.

"The woman went to Lincoln, but Sheriff Brady simply laughed at her and said there was nothing he could do. That is not a unique story and that is why there is celebration in this village when El Chivato sends one more of Jesse Evans's gang to the darkness in which he belongs."

The old man falls silent, and we sit and stare at each other. My brow is furrowed with worry as I try and make sense of all I have heard. It seems that the more I hear about Bill, the more people he becomes. Who is he: cold-blooded killer, or fighter on the side of the poor against power and corruption? A good singer and dancer who charms the *señoritas*, or a hardened leader of a gang of murderers? A hero or a villain? It depends on who you talk to or on what day you meet Bill.

"You look confused. The world is perhaps not as simple as you thought, or wished? That is the way of things. Have a drink, dance with a pretty girl and sleep. Tomorrow the world begins again."

I take the old man's advice and have a couple of glasses of the fiery mescal, dance with several brightly dressed girls and fall asleep in a bale of hay behind the livery stable. The next morning I discover something he didn't tell me. The mescal does make everything appear simpler, but the next morning the world begins again just as complicated as before. And my head hurts.

The heat of midmorning eventually forces me out of my bed of hay. I hold my aching head under the icy water of the horse trough until I am near drowned. Then I stagger over to complete the formalities of picking up the two horses. Even in my miserable state,

I can appreciate that these are good-looking beasts. One's a bay that reminds me a little of John Tunstall's poor animal. The other is a gray, almost white in places and flecked with a distinctive pattern of black. One half of its face is almost completely black, giving the impression that the horse is wearing a mask. These are mounts destined for officers.

I hitch the horses to the rear of the wagon and set off on the trail, ignoring several offers of a breakfast of tortillas and beans from a number of my dancing partners from the previous evening. It's April 5 and I am a bit behind schedule, but I'll make the best time I can and hope that Brewer will wait for me at Fort Stanton.

It's midafternoon before I approach Blazer's Mill. On the bright side, I'm feeling better and am even contemplating stopping for something to eat. The first thing I notice as I approach the mill is a small man standing staring into a hole in the ground. As I get closer, I notice that the hole looks suspiciously like a large grave. I dismount, hitch the mules to a rail and approach the man. He turns and looks at me suspiciously.

"Howdy," I say, smiling as broadly as I can. "What's going on?"

"Ain't you never seen a grave afore?" The man looks like a bird. He has a narrow pointed nose, and he looks at me with close-set, sharp eyes.

"I've seen graves before," I say. "Whose is this?"

The man spits on the ground. "Were a fight yesterday. Some Regulators come down to eat at Ma Godfroy's place. Best food this side of Santa Fe, if you want my opinion. If you're planning on eating, she has some wild turkey that'll have your mouth watering like Niagara Falls."

I don't want this man's opinion about food. The mention of Regulators being here rivets my attention. "What happened yesterday? Who was shot?"

The man looks momentarily annoyed at being interrupted but then launches into the story with gusto. "Round noon yesterday, 'bout six of them Regulator boys shows up to sup at Ma Godfroy's place. Like I said, her food's famous hereabouts."

"Was Bill Bonney with them?" I interrupt.

"Bill Bonney? You mean Kid Antrim? Sure he was with 'em. Him and a couple of the other boys been round here once or twice these past few weeks, asking after Jesse Evans. Kid were limping something fierce from a bullet wound in the leg.

"Anyways, as I was saying, they was just setting down to eat when Buckshot Roberts shows up. Now, I don't know whether you know this or not, young fella, but Buckshot used to ride with Jesse Evans. And Evans and his boys ain't too popular with the Regulators. Turns out that Buckshot was with the posse that rode out to McSween's place the day Tunstall were shot, and the Kid Antrim's carrying a warrant fer his arrest.

"Buckshot claims the warrant's been cancelled by Sheriff Brady, but the Kid just laughs and says that don't make no difference, 'cause old Bill Brady's been cancelled himself, and Buckshot better just surrender his gun and come quiet.

"Now, Buckshot says he ain't gonna do that 'cause that's the surest way to end up like Billy Morton and Frank Baker. Words was exchanged and then some shooting. John Middleton took a bullet in the chest and Frank Coe got his trigger finger shot clean off, but Buckshot took a killing shot right through the middle. Didn't die right away though. Holed up with his old Springfield rifle behind a mattress in the doorway of Godfroy's office yonder."

The small man points over to a large wooden house down by the river. "Now, Buckshot were dying, everyone including Buckshot knew that. He were yelling in pain and cussing the Regulators fit to bust. One of the Regulators took hisself over the creek to try and finish Buckshot off. Reckon Kid Antrim would've done it if it weren't fer his leg.

"The fella took a shot at Buckshot but missed. I reckon Buckshot saw the smoke, even though it were near a hundred and fifty yards off. He waited until the fella popped his head up fer another shot and fired. Shot him dead as that rock yonder. One of the nicest pieces of shooting I ever seen. So, this fella and Buckshot is both dead, though old Buckshot lingered, screaming until this morning. That's why we've gone and dug such a big hole. Aiming to bury them both together to save work."

The man falls silent, and I stand and stare into the hole. I'm angry that Bill's activities have caught up to me once more, yet also relieved that it wasn't him killed in the fight.

"The other Regulators still here?" I ask.

"Naw. They skedaddled soon as Buckshot killed their compadre. Didn't even stay to collect his body.

"That were some shot though," the man reflects appreciatively. "Hit the fella in the eye at a hundred and fifty yards, blew the back of his head clean off. You aiming on staying for the funeral?"

"No." My appetite's gone and I want to get as far from this new trouble as possible. Then I remember my promise to Lieutenant Fowler to find out about the mood on the reservation. "But I do have to speak to Frederick Godfroy."

"Fred'll be over yonder." The man nods back toward the wooden house.

"Thanks for the information," I say as I head away from the yawning grave.

⊹⇒

A number of men are standing in a group outside the house. Several turn to look at me as I approach.

"I'm looking for Mr. Godfroy," I say.

"He'll be in the parlor," one man volunteers.

I enter the front door and hear voices coming from the room to my right. I remove my hat and step through the doorway. Two crudely built open coffins are balanced on chairs. I glance into the closest one and see a body I don't recognize. I know most of the Regulators by sight and this man hasn't been shot in the head, so I assume it's Buckshot Roberts. I step over and look in the other coffin and a chill runs through me. The skin on the left side of the man's face sags unnaturally, as if the bones underneath have given up the struggle to hold the skin tight, and there's a gaping black hole where his eyes should have been, but there's no mistaking Dick Brewer.

My gasp brings over a middle-aged man with a kindly face.

"You know this fellow?" he asks.

I take a moment to recover from the shock and collect myself.

"Yes," I say. "He's Dick Brewer. He was John Tunstall's foreman."

"You a Regulator?" I sense the men in the room tense.

"No. I used to work for Tunstall is all. Brewer was a good man."

"Perhaps he shouldn't have come down here with the rest of those scum." I don't argue, and the man holds out his hand and introduces himself. "Fred Godfroy. Indian Agent on the reservation here. We're just about to put these boys in the ground if you want to stay and pay your respects. I can also offer you a bed for the night if you feel like breaking your journey, and that offer comes with a generous helping of Clara's famous turkey stew."

I think for a moment as I stare at Brewer's pale, mutilated face. Another man I counted as my friend dead. The calming influence and the only brake on Bill and the other hotheads is gone. I don't want to see him put in the ground with the man who killed him and I don't want a hearty meal and companionship. I need to escape and be on my own.

"Thank you for the offer," I say, looking at Godfroy's smiling face, "but I'll be on my way. I just stopped by on my way back to Fort Stanton because Lieutenant Fowler asked me to speak with you."

Godfroy nods and turns to the men in the room.

"Best get the lids on these boys and get them buried," he says before leading me outside. We move away from the gathered men down to the dry riverbed.

"Lieutenant Fowler wants to know the situation among the Apaches on the reserve," I say. "He's worried about trouble here."

"No doubt that these are difficult times," Godfroy begins, "and I'd be lying if I said there wasn't any tension among the young warriors here, but this isn't San Carlos. These are Mescaleros, not Chiricahuas. The land here-abouts is much more to their liking than the desert round San Carlos. And, thanks to Fowler and others like him, supplies arrive on time."

"I keep hearing that the reservation at San Carlos is so bad. Why?" I ask.

"Oh, it's bad all right. Hell's Forty Acres some call it. Back in '71, some genius decided it would be a good idea to collect all the Apache bands together on one reservation. I reckon it makes the paperwork easier for some fool behind a desk in Washington. But they made two mistakes. They picked the worst piece of land in Arizona Territory—barren desert, bad water and sickness. And they assumed all Apaches were the same. They ain't. Different bands live different lives, some like desert, but others, like Victorio, love mountains and trees. And there's not much of either at San Carlos.

"Victorio doesn't want a war. Only reason he goes off reservation is that we keep trying to send him to San Carlos. He's a Warm Springs Apache from Ojo Caliente. That's his sacred homeland. The government gave it to Victorio and his people 'for as long as the mountains stand and the rivers exist,' but I guess mountains don't last that long hereabouts. It was less than a year before the band was moved to San Carlos. That was the beginning of all the trouble with him. So far, he's only gone off reservation so he can return to Ojo Caliente, but if he ever declares war for real, God help us all.

"But listen to me harping on about old complaints. Right now things are not too bad here. I even hear word that Victorio might be sent here one day. It's not

Ojo Caliente, but it's better than San Carlos. He might go for it. I pray every night that he does."

Godfroy scans the surrounding hills as if he expects to see Victorio ride over them any minute. "So everything's quiet here?" I ask.

"As can be expected," Godfroy says, shifting his eyes back to meet mine. "I hear tales of mysterious comings and goings in the night. I suspect off-reservation warriors are coming in to try and persuade the young men to leave and join the fight. And a couple of them might. That one over there'll be first, I reckon." Godfroy waves a hand toward a small group of young Apaches, lounging in the shade of a pine tree. There are all dressed similarly in loose leggings tucked into calf-length buckskin boots and loose shirts. Their long dark hair lies on their shoulders and is held off their faces by broad colored headbands.

"That tall fellow in the middle of the group's bad news." One of the warriors is taller than the rest and stands stiffly, staring sullenly over at us. "His name's Ghost Moon, and I've had to warn him a number of times about stirring the others up. It wouldn't surprise me if we wake up one morning and he's long gone."

"Ghost Moon?" I ask, suddenly wrenched back to a barren hillside and my old friend Wellington telling me a story.

"It's what the Apache's call the full moon when it's out in daylight. You know him?"

I shake my head. "The name reminded me of a story I was told once."

"Well, stay clear of him. He's trouble, although I doubt many will leave with him when he goes. It's peaceful here and the food's relatively plentiful, so why exchange that for a hard, uncertain life on the run in faraway Texas and Mexico."

"So I can tell Lieutenant Fowler that everything is more or less peaceful and under control?"

"Peaceful for the moment, yes. Under control? If the band decides to kill me and Clara in our beds and walk away, there's no way I can stop them. However, I don't think that'll happen. The worst will be Ghost Moon and a couple of others, perhaps half a dozen at most, heading east to try their luck with whoever's off San Carlos at the moment."

From inside the house comes the sound of nails being hammered into coffin lids. I have to leave.

"Thank you," I say, moving back toward the house. "I'll pass what you said on to Lieutenant Fowler."

I load up some feed for the horses and mules and some jerky and beans for me and set off. I try not to look at the small group of men carrying the two boxes from the house to the gaping hole in the ground.

As I set off, I'm watched by the group of young warriors under the tree. I raise a hand in greeting as I pass. Several wave back, but Ghost Moon simply stands with his arms crossed, staring resentfully back at me. The hatred in his glare sends a shiver down my spine before his stare drifts back to the horses following along behind the wagon. I am glad when I have passed the group and am on my own once more.

I make camp by a rockfall at the mouth of a side canyon, a short way up the valley from Blazer's Mill. I tend to the mules and horses and build a fire at the base of a large rock as the sun lowers toward the western hills. Dinner is some jerked beef and a mug of coffee. I watch a large mesquite branch I have placed across the fire catch in the middle with a soft crackling sound and ponder the happenings of the past few days.

Lieutenant Fowler's mission was an escape from the helplessness I feel when I'm around Bill and the other Regulators. But there's no escape. I'm caught in a gunfight at Lincoln and just miss one at Blazer's Mill. Dick Brewer, the second friend I've made and lost since

I arrived here, is dead. Now there is no one to hold the Regulators in check and stop the killing. Going back to my safe home in Yale, as Wellington suggested, is looking more attractive. I've had all the adventure I can handle for the time being.

So that's what I'll do: take the horses up to Fort Stanton, go down and collect Coronado from McSween's ranch and head home.

But, as soon as I think that, doubts surface. Going home means getting on a boat and leaving Coronado, my one true friend. Also, this land has got under my skin. I've come to love the desert, its openness, its color, even the dryness. I love the contrast between the rugged, cactus-strewn hills and the green fertile flood-plains of the river valleys. It's all so different from the cool damp forests where I grew up.

Sometimes, as a boy, I used to feel that the forests were closing in on me. I would lie on a soft patch of moss, close my eyes and imagine the trees edging toward me, creeping nearer, trapping me. I used to scare myself doing this, but I always knew I was safe; all I had to do was open my eyes and the trees would be back where they were supposed to be.

Here, in the middle of a broad valley or on a hill-side, the landscape urges me to set off into it, to find out what is around the next bend in the river or across the next range of red hills.

This land makes me feel free. The only problem is the people. They are the danger, and they don't disappear when I open my eyes.

I pour the dregs of my coffee onto the dry ground at my feet. It disappears instantly into the sand. I look up at the sky. It's beautiful, the clouds painted blood-red near the horizon, washing out to the most delicate pink above my head.

I laugh ruefully to myself. In the course of a sunset I have convinced myself to go home and to stay here. So much for making a decision. With a sigh, I wrap myself in my poncho and settle beside the fire.

Something is wrong. I've gone from sleep to wakefulness instantly, but I don't know what has woken me. The branch has burned through and the glowing ends lie in the bed of coals that is what remains of my fire. I listen.

At first there is silence, but then I hear one of the horses whinny softly and shuffle its hooves. Is it being stalked by a mountain lion? Slowly I reach out for the branch lying in the fire. When I have a good grip, I throw the poncho off, stand up and shout.

Both horses whinny loudly. The light of a half moon shows me three human shapes frozen by the rear of the wagon. Before I even think of reaching for my gun, the largest figure yells and leaps at me. He has a painted war club raised, and for a big man he moves incredibly fast. I swing the branch at him. I miss, but the end flares up, revealing a glimpse of a face distorted by a scream, eyes wide and mouth open. It is Ghost Moon, the warrior Godfroy warned me about. I duck the first swing of his club, and we stand eyeing each other in the near dark.

One of the other men by the horses shouts something in Apache. I glance over and my opponent seizes his chance and lunges at me. I duck once more and thrust the burning branch up at his face. It strikes something and I hear a scream. Ghost Moon lets his club go in mid-swing and it sails over the fire and clatters against a rock. He staggers back, both hands clasping his face.

I drop the branch and reach for my revolver. As I draw and cock it, I become aware that there is only one man over by the horses. I just have time to wonder where the third man is, when an arrow shatters against the rock beside my head. I have to get out of the fire-light. Firing a wild shot into the darkness, I scramble away from the fire and into the rockfall. I'm clambering over a large jagged rock when the second arrow hits me. It only grazes my cheek, but I flinch and lose my footing. My right foot flies off the top of the rock and my thigh hits the rock as I fall. There's a loud *crack*, and I scream as pain shoots through my leg.

I end up huddled at the base of the rock with my left leg bent under me. My right leg is stretched out at an unnatural angle. I'm oddly calm. I know my leg is broken, but the initial searing pain has dulled to a strong ache. I'm oddly aware of everything. I can feel the warm blood trickling down my cheek and hear the *swish* as an arrow flies over my head. I'm still clutching my revolver, and I let off a shot toward the glow of the fire.

My shot is followed by some shouting and another arrow that clatters into the rocks to my left. I cock my gun and fire again. That only leaves two loads in the chamber. I decide to save them in case my attackers try to come over to finish me off.

I hear more voices, hoofbeats on the hard ground and then silence. I listen tensely for the sounds of someone creeping up on me, but there's nothing.

I don't know how long I huddle there in the rocks. My broken leg goes numb, but my left leg, bent awkwardly beneath me, begins to hurt. I realize that I can't stay here. Even if the warriors are gone, it could be days before anyone comes by and finds me, and I'll be dead long before that.

Taking a deep breath, I grip the rock beside me and begin to straighten my left leg. As I rise, my broken leg drags on the ground. I can feel bone ends grating against each other somewhere deep in my thigh. Waves of nausea sweep over me. I'm sweating profusely, yet I'm shivering with cold. But I have to keep going. If I don't, I'll die.

Inch by inch, I work my way around the rock. Eventually, with many stops and with tears of pain and frustration mixing with the blood on my cheek, I arrive behind the rock where I built my fire. There's a gap here with nothing to lean on. I reach over to the rock, but overbalance and fall. I land on my left side, but my broken leg flops to one side and the wave of pain forces another scream out of me before I black out.

I don't think I'm unconscious for long, but when I come to, all I want to do is lie where I am. I'm cold, but as long as I don't move, there's not much pain. If I just lie still, everything will be all right.

No, it won't! Move or die, those are my only choices.

Crawling on my good side, using my left arm to drag myself along, I finally make it around the rock to my fire. I scrape together some sticks that I had collected earlier and shove them onto the glowing coals. The small flames that lick around them and grow are the most comforting sight I've seen in my life. I haul my poncho over me, huddle as close as I dare to the warmth of the fire and fall asleep.

It's daylight when I open my eyes. I'm curled around the still-warm coals of my fire, so close that my poncho is singed. I lie still for a long time, working out what really happened last night and what is a fragment of the series of unsettling and confusing dreams that plagued what little sleep I managed to grab.

Ghost Moon and the other two were from the reservation, trying to steal the horses. My musings are disturbed by a soft bray. I twist my head to see the two mules standing a few feet away regarding me curiously. Behind them sits the wagon. There is no sign of the horses, which makes sense. Ghost Moon would want to move fast. The horses would help him, but the wagon and mules would just slow him down.

I'm ridiculously happy that I have survived the night, and now I have mules and a wagon. My problem is using them to get back to Blazer's Mill. I obviously can't do anything much with my broken leg flopping around. I look around for ideas.

The branch that I thrust into Ghost Moon's face is lying close by, the burned end black and cold. Perhaps there is a way I can immobilize my leg.

It takes a long time and causes a lot of pain to remove my belt. I realize that I've dropped my revolver somewhere in the rocks, but there's no way I'm going back to search for it. I cut wide strips off my poncho and rest. The next stage is going to be even less pleasant.

Collecting everything I will need close, I prop myself up on my left elbow. My good leg is fairly straight, and if I lean forward across the remains of the fire, I can reach close to my ankle without putting too much strain on my right leg, which lies beside it. I slip my belt and a couple of strips from my poncho under my left leg.

Now comes the hard bit. Reaching as far down as I can, I grab my right pant leg. I take a deep breath, count to three and haul my broken leg on top of my good one. My scream scares the mules, but it's done. I lie back, panting.

When the pain has subsided and my heartbeat returned to normal, I lean down, lay the branch alongside my broken leg and wrap the belt and poncho strips around everything. The belt I tighten close to my hips, above the break. The material I tie as best I can at my knee and as far down my calf as I can manage. It's cumbersome and far from perfect, and the knots are not as tight as I would like, but it'll be better than having my broken leg flopping around as I move.

I spend much of the rest of the day dragging myself over to the wagon, calling the mules over and crudely hitching them up. I talk to them constantly, thanking them for being such placid animals and so helpful. I promise them everything from their freedom to vast banquets of hay.

Finally, I manage to haul myself up onto the bed of the wagon. If I lie on my left side, as far forward as possible, I can see beneath the seat and give rough directions to the mules by hauling on the reins.

Despite the slow travel of the mules and all my precautions, every bump on the short journey back to Blazer's Mill is agony, but I'm insanely proud of my achievements. Despite everything, I haven't panicked or given in and just lain down. I've cheated death.

As I round the last hill and see Godfroy's house, I let out a weak cheer. The mules smell water and food and keep going even when I drop the reins and black out once more.

＝

"You're one lucky fella," Frederick Godfroy says as his wife, Clara, feeds me tiny spoonfuls of delicious soup. Whether I'm lucky or not can be argued both ways. I'm not lucky to have a broken leg, but I'm lucky not to be dead.

Last night, when the mules sauntered up and began drinking calmly at the trough, Godfroy came out to see why there was an empty wagon in front of his house. At first sight, with blood all over my face, he thought I was dead, but then I moved and cried out.

My crude attempt at a splint told him that my leg was broken, so he called a couple of men over and took the front door off the house to carry me in on. That short journey hurt as much as anything I had been through that day, as did removing the splint, cutting my pants off and Godfroy prodding to see what the damage to the bone was. Apparently I cursed him roundly and told him to leave me alone, but I remember very little until I woke up this morning in a makeshift bed in his parlor.

"Didn't think you'd appreciate being carried upstairs," he says with a smile as Clara holds my head and feeds me some more soup. "Far as could tell last night, the break's simple." He glances down at the two mounds made by my feet beneath the sheet that cover me. "Your right leg's about an inch shorter than the other, so I reckon, the bone ends are not matched up exact, but I'm not about to go pulling to try and set it better.

"I saw much worse in the war. With those splints I put on and a good long spell lying on your back, the bone ends should knit together well. I reckon you'll have a limp, but you should be able to get around all right."

"Thank you," I say weakly. "You saved my life."

"Nonsense. You did that. If you hadn't got yourself here, you'd most likely be buzzard food by now. What was I going to do, leave you outside in the wagon to smell the place up? If there's anything here that'll save your life, it'll be Clara's soup, so eat up.

"Now, you're more than welcome to stay here until you mend. I've sent a man off to Fort Stanton first thing this morning to let the army know that you're here and that those three have run off. I expect there'll be a patrol down here in a few days, and I asked for the fort surgeon to be with them, though I don't know there's much he can do that hasn't been already done. Meantime, you let Clara fuss over you."

"Thank you," I repeat. "The Apache that I burned last night, Ghost Moon, he watched me leave yesterday."

"I reckon he saw you with those two fine horses in tow and saw his chance," Godfroy says.

"If I hadn't woken up, he'd just have taken the horses and left."

"I doubt that. He's mean as they come. If you hadn't disturbed him, I reckon you'd have woken up with your skull caved in or your throat slit. I am a bit surprised that he didn't kill you for burning him like you say you did. Maybe you hurt him real bad or the others persuaded him not to. After all, the army'll put a lot more effort into catching a murderer than a horse thief.

"Still, it's the army's concern now, not ours. You just rest and let that leg heal."

I take the last spoonful of soup, and Clara nods in satisfaction. She wipes my chin and then hustles Godfroy out of the room to let me rest. My leg hurts constantly, but the warm soup feels good in my stomach and just feeling safe and knowing I don't have to drag my broken limb anywhere makes me feel ridiculously happy. Right now I can't think of anything better than lying on a makeshift bed in Godfroy and Clara's parlor. I drift off into a deep sleep.

14

"You're lucky," Lieutenant Fowler says. That's all I've heard for the last four days, how lucky I'm not a dried corpse beside a rock. I don't feel lucky. The euphoria I felt at not being out in the desert dragging a broken leg around has worn off. Even immobilized, I'm in constant pain, and every movement is agony. I haven't slept for more than an hour at a time since I got here. I'm exhausted, but as soon as I move in my sleep, the pain wakes me. I've failed the simple task I was set and I've lost everything, even my Father's revolver.

"I'm sorry I lost the horses," I say.

"Not your fault," Fowler says encouragingly, "though I daresay Colonel Dudley won't be happy. That gray with the black face-patch was for him."

"When are you setting off after them?"

"We're not. No point. They're long gone and the trail's cold. I sent a patrol south from Stanton when I heard what happened, hoping they might run into these boys as they head east, but it'll be sheer luck if they do. We're just here to show the flag, ride around the reserve a little to remind anyone thinking of following this Ghost Moon fellow that the army's about."

"Thank you for bringing the surgeon down."

"Least I could do, though I don't think he's been much help. Godfroy did a good job on you. You don't have an infection, and time's the only thing you need now. Surgeon reckons you'll be up and about by summer. You got plans for then? You going back to work for McSween?"

"No," I say. "At least I don't think so. Before I was attacked, I was thinking of going back home, up to Canada, but that doesn't feel right either."

Fowler regards me carefully for a long moment.

"Why do you not want to go back working for McSween?"

"McSween's a good man, but he's alone now. I just want to work, but with Tunstall and Brewer dead, the Regulators'll run wild. I've had enough of being caught up in this war. Everywhere I go, there's a fight and someone dies. Maybe I'll join the army."

I say it as a joke, but as soon as the words are out, the idea exists and Fowler isn't laughing.

"There's plenty fighting and dying if you're in the army."

"I know, but it would be my decision to become involved." As I talk, I begin to realize that I would like to ride with Fowler and his Buffalo Soldiers. It would be a simple life. "But I can't just become a soldier."

"That's true enough," Fowler agrees with a smile. "Even if you could get out of bed, you're not a Buffalo Soldier, but there are other ways. I expect that this summer we'll be busy sending patrols out after the renegades from San Carlos and Tularosa. It'll be hard, boring work. Usually the closest we get to the hostiles is finding a cold campfire or a dried-out body, but if you're interested, I can use some civilian scouts. We use friendly Apaches as trackers, but we also use men who know the country. To be honest, they're not much use—no one knows the country like the Apaches—but it's policy. I could probably get you taken on as a scout, if you're interested, and assuming your leg heals properly."

"I am," I say, so quickly it surprises me. I flinch as pain shoots through my leg.

The Lieutenant nods.

"I think we can use you, but there's nothing needs doing right now, and you've plenty time to think on things. I'll drop in whenever a patrol passes this way to see how the leg's healing. If you change your mind, just let me know. I won't take offence. It's a hard life and, if our patrols are successful, dangerous. The pay's poor and the food worse, but the men are good, and I guarantee you'll see a considerable amount of this country. You'll also need your own horse and equipment."

"That won't be a problem. My horse is being cared for over at McSween's ranch."

"All right." Fowler stands. "I'll check on your horse when we pass there on the way back. We'll talk more. For now you just need to heal."

As soon as I'm alone with my pain and my thoughts, I wonder what I've just done. The idea of becoming a scout for Lieutenant Fowler and his Buffalo Soldiers is attractive. I don't want to keep getting caught up in Bill's war, and I'm not ready to go home. It appears to be the perfect solution. The problem is that a scout needs to ride a horse, and it'll be a good two or three months before I can sit in a saddle. As Fowler said, I'll have plenty of time to reconsider.

⚡

April and May are the most boring months of my life. I can't move out of bed and yet the pain tires me dreadfully. Actually, the pain eases as my bone heals, but that makes the boredom worse. Clara has to nag me to keep me in bed. The highlight of that time is a slow, painful move to a proper bed in one of the rooms upstairs.

In early June, Clara lets me up for short walks each morning, but I sneak out of bed whenever possible and exercise. At first I'm as weak as a kitten and the pain is bad, but I persevere. I'm careful not to put too much weight on my leg or to fall, and gradually some strength comes back.

By the middle of June, I'm negotiating the stairs with the help of crutches and wandering around the yard. My progress speeds up now, and I celebrate Independence Day on July 4 by getting on a horse. It's a small pony. I do no more than walk around the house and I'm in pain all night as a result, but it's the first time I've been on a horse in almost three months. I've received no word from McSween's ranch, and I'm worried about Coronado.

On July 17, I'm riding around Blazer's Mill, thinking I'm ready for the journey to see Coronado, when a cavalry patrol descends from the hills. The Buffalo Soldiers have been around several times while I've been here, but never Lieutenant Fowler. This time, I'm delighted to see him leading the troop.

"Well, you're in better shape than when we last met," he says as he draws level and reins in. "Almost ready for work."

"I am," I say with a grin. I've done a lot of thinking over the past three months and I'm convinced that I want to be a scout for Fowler. It seems to solve all my problems.

"Excellent." Fowler returns my smile. "Let me settle the troop and wash some of this grime off, and we'll talk."

15

"Every day I get stronger," I say. Lieutenant Fowler and I are standing talking by the stable where the cavalry mounts are being tended. "I think the bone is fully healed. The only problem is that my right leg is about an inch shorter than the other. This gives me a bit of a limp, and my muscles are having to adjust. They ache if I try and do too much." Fowler looks at me and I hurriedly add, "But it doesn't stop me doing work."

"So, you're ready to become a scout for the Tenth Cavalry?"

"I am," I say confidently.

"Good. This patrol we're on now is just a ride through the reserve. It'll be later in the summer before we'll be heading into the hills, so you'll have time to work more on your fitness.

"A scout has to bring his own horse and equipment. Last I heard your horse was at the McSween place. I'll lend you a cavalry mount for now. If you're up to it, ride over there tomorrow, pick up your horse and gear and head up to Fort Stanton. I'll do my patrol round the reserve here, and when I get back, I'll talk Colonel Dudley into hiring you."

"Thank you," I say.

Fowler reaches into his pocket and hands me a worn letter. "This came for you a few days back. It sat in town for some time before the fellow there heard that we were headed down this way and sent it out to the fort."

The writing on the front of the letter says simply: *Jim Doolen, Lincoln, New Mexico Territory.* I recognize my mother's hand. As I hold this message from home, a thrill passes through me but also doubt. Am I doing the right thing becoming a scout for the army? I hurriedly stuff the unopened letter in my pocket and mumble thanks.

"What's been happening with the Regulators while I've been here?" I ask to distract myself from the letter.

"I hear stories from riders passing through of shoot-outs in the hills, but not too many details."

"That's pretty much all that's been going on. As far as I can see, everyone has warrants for everyone else's arrest. Evans leads a posse into the hills and the Regulators ambush them. The Regulators ride out and the posse ambushes them. Every time it happens the surgeon has to dig another bullet out of someone or a fresh grave has to be dug."

"Can't the army do anything?"

Fowler shakes his head. "I think Colonel Dudley would like to. He's in tight with Dolan and the new Sheriff, George Peppin. But we've got orders not to interfere unless we're fired on. I suppose it'll go on until everyone's dead or there's at least enough graves to persuade everyone that going on fighting is not worth it. Trouble is that most of these fellows on both sides only know how to use a gun. They wouldn't know what to do if there were no war going on."

I imagine Bill being chased around the hills or lying in ambush behind a rock, all the while with a smile on his face. For all the charm that drew me to him when we first met, I suspect that Bill is one of the men Fowler is talking about, only happy with a gun in his hand.

"But the Regulators are not your concern now," Fowler says. "You're almost a scout. Go and see Sergeant Rawlins and say that I've authorized a mount and equipment for you to transport back to the fort."

"Thank you," I repeat. "I promise I'll be a good soldier." I attempt a crude salute.

Fowler laughs.

"Three things. You won't be a soldier, you'll be a scout. And in the cavalry the men aren't called soldiers but troopers. And civilians don't salute."

"S-sorry," I stammer, feeling my face redden with embarrassment at making such a fool of myself.

"And don't ever say sorry. You think about what you're going to do, do it and live with the consequences. You do that and we'll get along fine. Now go and see Sergeant Rawlins."

Fighting down the instinct to attempt another salute, I limp over to where the cavalry horses are tethered.

―――

"She ain't the liveliest beast, and I wouldn't want to be on her back if I were being chased by a band of Apaches on those fast little ponies they ride, but she'll get you to McSween's place." Sergeant Rawlins is introducing me to a brown and white pinto mare who's standing in her stall, chewing contentedly.

"What's her name?" I ask.

"She ain't got a name," Rawlins says. "Troopers do name their mounts, but this'un's a spare. Call her what you wish. Her saddle and tack's hanging on the fence yonder." Rawlin's glances at my belt. "You be needing a side arm? We got some Cavalry Colts. You can have one."

"Thank you," I say. Rawlins is my height but broad across the shoulders. His short curly hair is tinged with gray at the edges, but the wrinkles on his face all come from smiles, and I instinctively like him. I remember Fowler saying that he had fought in the Civil War.

"Go and draw rations for the ride from Godfroy, and I'll meet you back here. You've got a good few hours of daylight left, and I expect you'll want to make a mile or two."

I do as I'm told and think as I do it that this is probably a good characteristic for a soldier—a trooper, I correct myself. And for a scout too.

Rawlins takes a long-barreled revolver out of the holster he is carrying.

"You used one of these afore?" he asks.

"No," I reply. "My Colt Pocket revolver was smaller."

"Then this is how you do it." Rawlins pulls the hammer back to half cock and opens the section behind the chambers on the right side. He takes a handful of bullets from the box he has brought and feeds them in as he rotates the cylinder. He closes the section and lowers the hammer and hands it to me. It's surprisingly heavy.

"Easy," he says. "Just cock the hammer, pull the trigger and you'll blow a sizeable hole in anyone who gets in the way."

The rations are basic: some hard biscuits and some tough-looking jerky. Not nearly as appetizing as Clara's meals. And they don't come close to filling the two large army saddlebags that I strap onto the pinto. The saddlebags are emblazoned with a crest showing two bison.

"Buffalo Soldiers," Rawlins comments when he sees me examining the crest. "Most folks think it's because of the hair." He smiles and rubs the top of his head. "But that ain't it. It's 'cause a cornered buffalo never gives up until it's stone dead. We're the same."

"Lieutenant Fowler told me the story of Private Randall and the Cheyenne war party."

Rawlins nods. "But did he tell you why we never give up?"

"He didn't."

"It's 'cause we got nothing to lose. Most of these boys're ex-slaves, either escaped or freed at the end of the war. Only freedom they've ever known has been in the Tenth Cavalry. Same for the boys in the Ninth. They'll die for that freedom."

"But they wouldn't be slaves outside the army either," I point out.

"You ever been to New York?"

I shake my head.

"Well, it ain't like the slavery in the plantations down south, but it's slavery just the same." Rawlins smiles broadly at my puzzled look and continues. "Mr. Fowler's a good man, got an education and all, but most of the troopers in this outfit ain't got no book learning. If they weren't in the army, what would they do?"

Rawlins answers his own question before I have a chance to say anything. "They'd do the worst jobs there is for the meanest bosses and the lowest wages. Trooper Elroy escaped from a plantation in Alabama in '64 after he was beat so bad the foreman broke three of his ribs. He made it north to New York and the promised land. He weren't owned by no one for the first time in his life, but he were hated."

"Why?" I asked. "By whom?"

"By the Irish. See, the Irish gangs controlled all the low jobs and kept them for their own. They saw the free slaves as a threat, taking those jobs away from them 'cause they would work for even less. Elroy says that he never met hatred on the plantation like the hatred he felt in New York. Anyway, he got work. He can't read two words nor write a letter, so he was putting in twelve or fourteen hours a day in the slaughterhouse for barely enough money to put a roof over his head, food in his belly and soap enough to wash the blood off every evening. On top of that, he had to crawl halfway home each night to avoid being beaten to death by the Irish. The Tenth Cavalry's as close to the Lord's Paradise as Elroy's going to get on this earth. He'll die for it afore he goes back to that New York slaughterhouse."

"I see," I say, as I ponder another of life's unexpected complexities.

"Now you get your equipment loaded and get on the trail. We'll see you back at the fort. And try not to run into any Apaches."

Rawlins turns away.

"Alita," I say.

"What's that?" Rawlins says as he turns back.

"That's what I'll call the pinto," I explain, stroking the mare's neck. "I had a horse by that name once."

Rawlins nods and leaves. I step to Alita's head.

"Do you like the name, Alita?" I ask softly. Alita tosses her head gently. "I used to have a horse by that name, but she was shot and killed. It's a strong name. Alita was a girl who fought in the war for Mexican independence from Spain." The mare whinnies softly and nuzzles my neck. "I'll take that as a yes," I say. "But now we have to get going."

I saddle Alita and swing the saddlebags into place. I walk over to the Godfroy house to say my thank-yous and farewells. Fred, as I've come to know him, shrugs off my thanks, wishes me well and shakes my hand firmly. Clara fusses about my leg and gives me a bag of fresh baked biscuits for the trail. I'm sorry to leave these kind, generous people and promise to drop by when I get the chance.

Forcing myself not to flinch at the pain, I mount Alita and set off, hoping that this new beginning means I can leave Bill and the war I've been caught up in behind. But am I making the right choice? My mother's unopened letter weighs heavily in my pocket.

16

I sit by a fire, a good long ride from Blazer's Mill. This is the farthest I've ridden in months, and I'm pleased with my progress. My leg aches, but the pain is manageable. I should make McSween's ranch in good time tomorrow. I'm excited about seeing Coronado once more.

I pull the letter out of my pocket and stare at it for a long time before I unfold it. I'm nervous. No sooner have I made a decision about what to do—scout for Lieutenant Fowler—than this message arrives from the past, the first I have heard from home in almost a year. How much has changed, how much I've changed, in that time. It was a letter from my father that got me into all this in the first place. Will what my mother has to say now make me regret what I have committed to? There's only one way to find out.

Dearest Jim,

I was so excited to get your letter from Mexico.

The news that your father has been dead all these years comes as no surprise. I have always known that, if it were possible, he would have contacted me somehow, so I suspected the worst. I knew some of what you told me about his past, but he was a man of few words and what you say has filled in many blank spots. I never suspected the complexity, or tragedy, of his background. You do not say much about your role in the events you describe. I hope you did nothing that you are ashamed of.

Don't worry about me. Things are good here in Yale. In fact, I have some exciting news for you.

Do you remember Sam Billings who runs the general store? His wife's been dead these past five years and I have always suspected that he took a liking to me. Well, he has begun to pay court and last week he asked for my hand and I accepted.

It is not the romantic love match talked about in the dime novels you used to read, but he is a decent, sensible man and it is not a good thing to grow old alone. It is our intention to sell the stopping house, and I will help Sam in the store. I hope that we will have your blessing.

I was not surprised that you decided not to come directly home from Mexico and instead see some of the world. I have always said that you shared your father's restless spirit. I wish you well on your journeys. Write when you can and come and visit Sam and me when you are able.

I will send this to Lincoln where you say you are headed and hope that it reaches you soon. You're a good boy and sensible enough to stay out of trouble. Be careful and know that my best wishes, and Sam's, go with you wherever you are.

With love,

Mary

I read the letter three times in the firelight, each time swallowing back tears. I'm happy that my mother is going to get married again. I remember Sam Billings well. He's a round, jovial man who always had a hard candy or a glass of sasparilla for us kids. Mom will be happy with him, but it means that I now have no reason to go home. In fact, I have no home to go to. Yale could only ever offer me my mother and the stopping house, and now she will be married to Sam and the stopping house sold.

I know I chose not to go home after Casas Grandes. And I accepted scouting for Lieutenant Fowler just hours ago. But now I feel cut adrift. I am truly on my own. I rub my aching leg, curl up by the fire and try to sleep.

—✦—

"Where's my horse?" I grab the man standing by the corral at McSween's ranch. A line of open horse stalls has been built along one side since I was last here; all but one are empty.

"I don't know?" he says, nervously. "Who're you?"

"I'm Jim Doolen. My horse is Coronado, the one with the white star on his forehead. I left him here when I went on an errand for McSween back in April. Where is he?"

"Don't know," the man says and begins to edge away. I grab him by the collar and push him hard against the stable wall. I'm so angry that I hardly know what I'm doing, but my gun is suddenly out of its holster and pressed into the man's ribs. Close up, I see that he's a kid, barely older than me. His eyes are wide with fear.

"Don't shoot me, mister," he whines. "I didn't take your horse."

I put my gun away, ashamed at having threatened him, and release his shirt. He's not a cowboy, his hands are smooth and he's wearing city clothes.

"I'm not going to shoot you. I just want to know what happened to my horse."

"Bill took him," the boy says.

"Why?"

"Don't rightly know. That horse was a problem, wouldn't let anyone ride him. Bit if you got too close. Bill took it as some kind of a challenge. Worked him hard out in the corral until he could ride him. Took him out with most of the boys a few days back. Mr. McSween went with them, said he was scared to stay here without any protection." The boy glances around nervously.

"Did Bill hurt my horse?"

The boy lowers his eyes.

"Did he hurt my horse?" I repeat, stepping forward.

"Not much," the boy says hurriedly. "Just used the crop a bit to show it who was boss."

I curse under my breath.

"Where'd Bill take him?"

"Don't know," the boy says, "honest. Bill and the Regulators set off early in the morning. Never said where they were going or when they'd be back. I heard them talk the night before about recruiting some Hispanics who don't like Dolan."

My first instinct is to mount Alita and ride off after Bill, but that would be stupid. I have no idea where he is. Did they go to La Luz, Picacho, San Patricio, or up to Roswell? It would be like looking for a needle in a pile of hay.

"What's your name?"

"Harvey. Harvey Morris."

"You a Regulator?"

"No, I'm a law student. I knew Alex McSween out east. I told him I had the consumption, and he wrote and invited me out here. Said the dry air was good for the lungs and that there was plenty opportunity and I could study under him. Said he'd make me a partner. I didn't expect all this trouble."

"Neither did I," I say. "I'm sorry I threatened you."

"That's okay," Harvey says with a slight smile. He's taller than I am but very thin, with high, prominent cheekbones, light blue eyes and pale skin.

"I've got to head up to Fort Stanton, but I'll be back in a few days. If Bill comes back while I'm gone, tell him I was here and that I want Coronado back, unharmed."

I'm angry at Bill for taking Coronado and for hurting him with the crop, but I'll say nothing if I get my horse back. I know better than to go up against Bill. I've learned that's a good way to end up dead. I mount Alita.

"You headed up through Lincoln?" Harvey asks.

I nod.

"Might I ride along with you?" Harvey looks down at his boots in embarrassment. "To be honest, being here alone is frightening. There's not much stock left, and the few cowboys around can easily look after them. I could stay at McSween's house in town. His wife, Susan, lives in it." He looks up at me. "Company's always better on the trail, don't you think?"

I don't think that. I'd rather be on my own. The last thing I want is to play nursemaid, but Harvey looks at me with such a pleading expression that I haven't the heart to turn him down. He's a city boy, fresh from the east, and probably he's spent the past few days imagining either Jesse Evans riding onto the ranch and shooting him, or a band of wild Indians sneaking up behind him with scalping knives clenched between their teeth. He looks terrified.

"All right," I say, "but get ready quick and you'll need to keep up." With me riding Alita, the slowest horse I've ever been on, the last instruction doesn't mean much unless Harvey intends to walk to Lincoln.

"Thank you," Harvey says as he turns and runs to the only occupied stall to saddle his horse.

As I wait for Harvey, I think back on what he said. Bill and the others have gone out to recruit Hispanics to fight with the Regulators. Given what the old man in La Luz told me about how the people there felt about Dolan, I doubt they'll have much difficulty. But why? Does Bill have something planned? I have a sudden feeling that things are rushing toward some sort of conclusion, and I pray that I can avoid it.

⊬⊐

The main street of Lincoln is deserted as Harvey and I ride into town late in the afternoon on July 18. It's only nine miles to Fort Stanton, but Alita and I are both thirsty and my leg's hurting fiercely, so we stop at the horse trough outside the small courthouse beside Squire Wilson's house. Alita drinks gratefully and I enjoy washing some of the trail dust off my face.

Harvey doesn't dismount but sits and glances nervously between the building beside us and up the street, where the Tunstall store and McSween's house are just visible in the distance.

"Howdy." I look up. The man standing behind me is only middle-aged, but his hair is white. His bushy mustache and goatee stand out brightly against his weather-beaten skin. He looks vaguely familiar. I nod a greeting.

"That's a cavalry mount you got there," he says, regarding the buffalo insignia on the saddlebags.

"It is. I'm taking it to Fort Stanton to deliver to Lieutenant Fowler."

"I see. And after you deliver it, how you aiming to get home?"

It's a good question.

"I don't know. I was going to bring my own horse, but someone else took it."

"That's bad luck for you. Can I see the papers you got from this Lieutenant Fowler?"

"He didn't give me any papers." I'm beginning to feel nervous at the questioning. Who is this man?

"I see," the man repeats. "Now this presents me with a difficulty. There's been quite a bit of horse thieving these past few weeks, and here you are riding a cavalry horse that you say you're delivering to Fort Stanton, yet you got no horse of your own to ride home on and no official signed papers."

"I'm no horse thief," I say. "I'm telling you the truth. Who are you anyway?"

"I'm sorry," the man says with a smile that borders on a leer. "Name's George Peppin. Folks call me Dad, 'cause of my white hair and all. I'm the Sheriff hereabouts."

Now I realize where I've seen this man before. He was one of the deputies with Sheriff Brady the day of the ambush just up the street. He must be Brady's replacement, which means he's a Dolan man. I get a sinking feeling in the pit of my stomach.

Peppin's smile broadens but doesn't become friendly.

"Would you be one of them Regulator trash?"

"No," I say, as convincingly as I can manage. "Like I said, I work for Lieutenant Fowler. I'm going to be scouting for him when he rides out after the Apaches who ran from the reservation down at Tularosa Canyon."

"That right? Well, I don't reckon that's the whole truth. I reckon you are a Regulator come here to help them others out, and what's more, I reckon you are a horse thief." Without me noticing, Peppin has drawn his gun and now it's in his right hand, pointing at my stomach. "See, I recognize you. You're the fella who walked across the street here, bold as you please, right after Bill Brady and George Hindman was murdered in cold blood."

Harvey's horse skitters sideways up the street, but Peppin ignores it.

"I wasn't part of that," I plead, unable to take my eyes off the unwavering muzzle of Peppin's revolver. "I was just passing through town, taking supplies to Fort Stanton. I went over to see what was happening and got caught there when the shooting started."

"My, my. Always on your way to Fort Stanton and never part of any of the trouble that happens around you. You sure are one unlucky fella, a good one for the stories too. Next you'll be telling me that you're Colonel Dudley himself. Now you just hand me that Colt on your belt, real easy, and we'll take a walk up the street to the jail and you can rest from all your journeying while we sort this out."

For a long moment I stand and stare at Peppin and his gun, trying desperately to think of something I can do to get out of this mess. Something he said sticks in my mind. "What others? You said, you reckoned that I was in town to help the other Regulators. What did you mean? Are there Regulators in town?"

Peppin glances up the street. As if on cue, there's a burst of gunfire from the direction of McSween's house.

Harvey's horse rears as its rider jerks the reins in fright. Harvey tumbles to the ground and the horse gallops off down the street.

Peppin looks uncertain, his revolver wavering between Harvey and me. A bullet from up the street chips the edge of the horse trough and whines into the air. Peppin makes up his mind. He grabs Alita's reins and, keeping her between him and the firing, retreats toward the court-house. I take a step after him but the loud *click* of his revolver being cocked stops me in my tracks. Another bullet kicks up dust at Peppin's feet and, dragging Alita's reins, he runs for cover around the side of the building.

Harvey's on his feet now, looking around nervously. I feel naked standing out in the middle of the street, but where to run to? I notice a movement and look up to see a figure with a rifle in the courthouse window. At the same time I hear a familiar voice behind me, "This way. Get over here."

Without further encouragement, I grab Harvey's sleeve and set off in a limping run across the street. I hear shots behind me but don't know if they're aimed at us or not.

Harvey and I tumble behind a broken adobe wall to find Bill standing with his revolver drawn, smiling. He lets off two quick shots across the street.

"I've missed you, Jim, lad, but you sure picked an awkward time to come visiting." A bullet thuds into the wall. "But I reckon we'd best save the pleasantries for later. Follow me."

As dusk falls, we follow Bill along the backs of the buildings facing onto the street, dodging along walls and fences and sprinting between the cover of outhouses, barns and sheds. There is sporadic firing all around, but none of it seems aimed at us. Eventually, we burst through the back door of a large adobe house into a big kitchen, where half a dozen men look up at our arrival. "Bill," one of them says, "you're back just in time for the party."

"Always liked a party," Bill replies.

"What's going on?" I ask Bill after the banter has stopped.

"Lots happened while you been relaxing down at Blazer's Mill. We've shot some of theirs, and they've shot some of ours. No one's backing down, so we figured it was time to resolve this for good.

"All the boys got together and rode down through San Patricio, La Luz and Picacho. Lot of Hispanic boys down there ain't too fond of Dolan and the high prices he charges. Anyone with a grudge was welcome to join us. I reckon we doubled our strength in that one ride. Must be fifty or sixty all told now.

"We rode in four days back, planning to ambush Evans and his posse as they rode into town the next day and take Lincoln back from these thieves and crooks, but it didn't work. Someone must've seen us setting up. Anyway, they set up down the street in the hotel and Dolan's store. Been shooting at each other on and off ever since."

"Is McSween here?"

"Sure, everyone's here."

"And where's Coronado?"

A puzzled expression flits over Bill's face; then he laughs.

"That's one mean horse, but we came to an understanding."

"You'd better not have hurt him."

"Or what?" Anger flashes across Bill's face, but then his smile returns. "No damage done. He just needed to be shown who was in charge."

I decide not to push it any further.

"Where is he now?"

"In the corral behind the house with the other mounts." Bill jerks his thumb at the back door.

"I'm going to check on him," I say. Bill shrugs.

I'm excited to see Coronado again. I've come to be very fond of Alita, but Coronado is my friend.

Darkness has fallen while I was talking to Bill, but I have no trouble finding the horses and Coronado.

"Are you all right?" I stroke Coronado's neck, and he nuzzles me affectionately. "Bill didn't harm you, did he?" The horse whinnies quietly. "Well, we'll be out of here soon. I don't want to go riding about the country-side on a moonless night like this. I'll stay the night at the house. At first light I'll come and get you and we'll see if we can find Alita. I imagine Peppin put her in the livery stable. You'll like her, she's a cavalry mount. Then we'll head out to Fort Stanton. I've got us work as scouts with the cavalry. That'll keep us a long way from the troubles going on in Lincoln."

I go on to tell Coronado the story of my adventures at Blazer's Mill, my injury and recovery. Ever since Wellington talked to Coronado, I've done the same. It's comforting and companionable, and he seems to like it, standing quietly and nuzzling my shoulder.

"We'll be away from all this soon," I say. "It'll be good to be out on the trail where life's so much simpler."

With a final stroke of Coronado's neck, I leave him with the other dozen or so horses and feel my way through the blackness to McSween's house.

nside the house there's a festive atmosphere. A fire crackles in the parlor grate and lanterns dispel the shadows in every corner. Bill stands by the fire, playing a harmonica, and another man is squeezing out a rough tune on a small concertina. The air is a blue haze of tobacco smoke, and everyone is either stamping their feet in time to the tune or humming loudly along.

There are more than a dozen people standing around; some I recognize as Regulators, others are strangers. I see McSween and Harvey sitting at a table with a dark-haired woman. I decide to go over and tell McSween what happened to me, but before I can move, a hand catches my arm.

"*Buenas noches, joven.*" I turn around to see the old man from La Luz who told me the story of Davy Crockett at the Alamo.

"What are you doing here?" I ask in surprise.

"I have come to fight," he says proudly, patting a pair of antiquated flintlock pistols stuffed into his belt. "Perhaps we shall be heroes together, no? But first I must sing a *corrido.*"

Bill and the concertina player have stopped, and the old man steps forward. With no accompaniment, he begins singing in Spanish in a wavering voice. Surprisingly, Bill joins in.

> *"Atención pido a la gente,*
> *pido por última vez,*
> *adiós compadres amados*
> *del finado.*
> *Adiós compadres amados*
> *del finado Manuel Maés."*

I struggle to follow the story. It seems to be about the death of a famous buffalo hunter called Manuel Maés. Each verse has him saying farewell to his family, friends and his life.

When he finishes, the old man bows theatrically and is rewarded with scattered applause.

"Let's have a dance," someone shouts out, and Bill launches into a vigorous tune and someone produces a guitar and joins him. Soon, everyone is foot-tapping and several men are clumsily attempting to dance in the confined space. I slip around the edge of the crowd.

"Hello, Mr. McSween," I say.

McSween looks up at me. He appears tired and distracted, and there are gray bags under his eyes as if he hasn't slept in several days. It takes him a moment to recognize me.

"Jim, isn't it?" he says. I nod. "Good to see you back to lend a hand. Have you met my wife, Susan?" He indicates the woman sitting beside him. She's well-dressed and wears her hair up and held in place with pins and lace ribbons.

"Pleased to meet you, ma'am," I say. She smiles back and her face lights up. She looks me straight in the eye with a confident gaze.

"Harvey's been telling of your meeting with Peppin," McSween says.

"We had no idea what was going on in town and rode into the middle of it," I say. "I don't know what would have happened if Bill hadn't got Harvey and me out of it."

McSween looks thoughtful.

"I was wrong," he says.

"What do you mean?"

He looks up at me with his tired eyes.

"I thought there was a legal way, a civilized way, to resolve all this. But to reach a civilized solution, you have to be dealing with civilized men. Bill was right all along—the only answer to all of this will come out of a gun. Perhaps if I'd accepted that earlier, fewer good men would be dead now."

Susan reaches over and strokes McSween comfortingly on the back. He turns to her and forces a weak smile. He looks over at Harvey.

"I'm sorry I brought you into all this."

"It's all right, Mr. McSween. It'll all be over soon, and then we can get back to practicing law." His words are confident, but his voice wavers with uncertainty.

"I think I have chosen well for my future partner," McSween says, and Harvey grins so wide I think his face will split. "Enjoy yourself tonight," McSween adds. "I have a feeling there will be business to attend to in the morning."

I don't want to tell McSween that I'm leaving at first light, so I simply nod and move back across the room. Bill has finished playing and joins me. His face is flushed and gleams with sweat. I am still angry with him and have been around him enough now to know not to trust his charm, but I don't say anything. I don't want any trouble before I can slip away.

"There's nothing like those Mexican dance tunes for working up a sweat," Bill says.

"How many Regulators came with you?" I ask.

"When we rode into town, about sixty, counting the Hispanics," Bill replies. "Some have slipped away in the past few days, but there's still enough good men for what we need to do. About fifteen here and a few more over at Tunstall's store, Montano's and Ellis's places."

"Will this end the war?"

"Sure will. But we've got to move quick tomorrow. Only a matter of time afore the army intervenes. We got to hit Evans and the rest hard, drive them out of town. Then we'll stroll over to the Dolan store and help ourselves to what we want." Bill winks at me. "The problem's solved."

I'm amazed that Bill seems to believe what he is saying. Has he learned nothing in the past six months? How does he imagine his thirty or so men will move

at least that number of Dolan men out of their forti-
fied positions around town? Even if they do succeed,
Dolan has a lot of friends in high places with a financial
stake in his contracts for the army. I doubt they will sit
quietly by. But it's not my problem. Soon I'll be gone,
off on the trail scouting for Lieutenant Fowler.

"I'm going to find myself somewhere to lie down,"
I say. "It's been a long day and my leg bothers me."

"Dancing's the best thing for a bad leg," Bill says.
"I reckon I'm ready for another tune." He flashes me a
sly look. "There's space down in the cellar if you want
to escape the noise."

I say my thanks, grab a lantern and find the steps
down to the cellar. The room is dry and pleasantly
cool, and I look around in the wavering light. Shadows
dance around the piles of boxes and odds and ends.
I see a dusty wardrobe and a couple of large travel
trunks. There's no bed, but there is a long dining table
at the far end of the room. There's stuff piled on it and
covered with a blanket. It will do for the few hours'
sleep I need before I can leave.

I cross the room, being careful not to trip on the
uneven floor. Without looking, I haul the blanket off
whatever's on the table. My cry of surprise brings gales
of laughter from the stairs up to the house. There's the

body of a man on the table. His eyes are open, staring at nothing, and there's a dark blood-encrusted hole in the side of his head.

"Say hello to Tom Cullins." I hear Bill's voice, rich with humor, from behind me. "Old Tom passed too close to a window this morning. He didn't feel too much like joining the party, so we put him down here so's he wouldn't smell the place up too bad."

Now I understand the look Bill gave me when he suggested I find a place to sleep down here. He knew I'd find the body, and he and some others followed me down the stairs to see the reaction.

Fighting to control my temper, I push past Bill and the others on the stairs. I find a chair as far from the revels as I can and slump into it. I can't wait to escape from this place.

18

The fusillade of gunshots wakes me instantly, and I open my eyes to a cloud of dust hanging in the gray dawn light. Without thinking, I roll off the chair, grab my revolver and scramble through to the parlor.

Men are running everywhere, falling over each other and trying to keep away from the windows. Bullets are thudding into the thick adobe walls. As I burst into the room, a bullet crashes into the wall beside my head and Bill yells, "Get down."

I fall to the ground and crawl over to crouch beside the window. Bill is on the opposite side, peering carefully out of the corner. He is holding his Colt fully cocked.

"Army's here," he says without taking his eyes from the street outside. "Must've got into town last night."

"But the army's not allowed to interfere," I say, remembering what Lieutenant Fowler told me.

"They can if someone shoots at them."

"You shot at a soldier?" I ask, horrified.

"Not me," Bill says casually. "One of the other fellas couple of days back. Soldier was poking around out there. Obviously Peppin sent for him, so we fired a couple of warning shots. Never come close to hitting him." Bill lifts his revolver and fires off a couple of quick shots out the window. A fusillade of bullets thump into the wall in return. When it stops, I risk a glance into the street.

There are glimpses of men moving in the buildings across the street. There are also some on the roofs and taking cover behind wagons and horse troughs. There appear to be a lot of them, but what frightens me most is the scene at the end of the street. There's a squad of soldiers gathered around a howitzer, and it's pointed right at us.

"They've got a cannon," I say breathlessly as I slip back down.

"They got a Gatling gun as well," Bill says nonchalantly. "Just for show. They won't use them."

Bill doesn't sound unduly bothered by the situation. He may even be right, but I'm not staying to find out. Keeping low, I cross the parlor and into the kitchen. Susan McSween and Harvey are in there, huddled in a corner. I open the back door.

Two things happen before I've taken two steps. I see several men untying Coronado and the Regulator horses and a bullet catches the flap of my jacket and thuds into the wall behind me. I throw myself to my right, behind a rain barrel as two more bullets whistle by. I'm breathing heavily and I can feel sweat forming on my back.

I cock my revolver and peer around the barrel. I can see a man leading a protesting Coronado away, but I don't dare shoot for fear of hitting my friend. A bullet splashes into the barrel, spraying me with water. There's no way I can get to the horses and escape, and it's equally obvious that I can't stay here. I reach over the barrel and fire off a couple of shots blind; then I throw myself back at the kitchen door and pile onto the floor.

"There's no way out," Harvey says as I catch my breath. "We're trapped. There's nothing we can do."

"Nonsense." Susan McSween stands up. "There's always something we can do."

"Get down," Harvey yells, but Mrs. McSween ignores him. She strides through the house toward the front door. Keeping low to the ground, I follow her.

As she reaches for the door handle, Bill sticks his head out of the parlor. "What're you doing? Don't be crazy. They'll shoot you."

Susan McSween ignores him, pulls the door open and steps out into the morning sun. Bill and I rush to the door and peer out.

Miraculously, as Mrs. McSween walks forward, holding herself straight and lifting her skirts out of the dust, the firing on both sides falls away and, finally, stops completely. Everyone watches in silence as the brave woman strides onto the street, stops and looks around. An officer I don't recognize, steps out from the army position and approaches. The pair talks for a moment, and then Mrs. McSween sets off down the street with him.

"Susan!" McSween appears in the hallway and tries to barge past Bill and me. We hold him back. Outside, his wife ignores his shouted pleas and keeps walking. Eventually, McSween gives up his struggle and sags down against the wall. "It's all gone to hell," he mumbles miserably. "John and Dick both dead, and we'll be next."

"Quit whining," Bill says harshly.

"I'm sorry," McSween mumbles, but whether he means for whining or getting us into this mess isn't clear.

"You should be sorry." Bill's eyes have narrowed and he's leaning close to McSween's face. "If you'd had more guts after Tunstall was murdered, we could have ended this then."

"I'm a lawyer," McSween says, "not a gunfighter."

"A coward is what you are."

McSween flinches as if hit.

"That's not fair, Bill," I say. "If anything made this mess worse, it was you and the Regulators and your blind desire for revenge." I'm angry. Here I am once again, stuck in a situation that I had no part in creating and that I want no part of, and again, Bill's at the heart of it.

"What do you know, Canada boy," Bill spits at me, pushing forward until his face, twisted in rage, is inches from mine. "You take no part in our fight. You got no right to say anything."

"I've got a right," I say. "I want no part of your killing, but it's everywhere. Whenever I turn, there's you, and then someone dies."

"You're a coward," he yells at me. "Just like McSween here." Bill pushes me hard in the chest and I crash back painfully into the wall. Instinctively, I swing at him and feel pain as my fist connects with his jaw.

Bill staggers back, surprised. He raises his hand to his lip and it comes away bloody. As if by magic, his Colt is in his hand, the black muzzle pointing unwaveringly at my face. The click of the hammer cocking sounds deafening.

For an age we stand staring at each other. I've seen Bill's rage and know that if I make the slightest wrong move, I'll be dead before my body hits the floor.

"There's plenty outside to fight without us killing each other." I see Harvey out of the corner of my eye. I keep watching Bill, praying that he won't be able to shoot someone who is looking him in the eye.

The gun barrel rises and the hammer clicks off. Suddenly, Bill is smiling broadly.

"Never thought you'd do that," he says. "Maybe you ain't such a coward after all."

I remain silent and Bill moves away into the parlor. I turn to Harvey. "Thanks." He smiles shyly. I take a deep breath to calm my nerves and head down to the cellar. I need somewhere quiet to think.

I sit in the dark cellar all morning, the dead Tom Cullins my only company. I feel helpless, like Ishmael in *Moby Dick*, trapped on the *Pequod* by the maniacal Captain Ahab's overwhelming desire for revenge. Every turn I take in my story leads me back to Bill and his murderous intent. At every corner, I find him standing just out of sight, smiling as he plans another death. Wellington warned me that we do not always have control over our stories and where they take us, and I should have listened to him. What will rescue me from this?

All morning I hear thumping feet, shouts and gunshots above me. It must be early afternoon when I first smell the smoke. The firing appears to have stopped, so I go up to investigate.

The McSween house is built with two wings extending from the main building. One wing is filled with smoke and the wooden timbers supporting the adobe walls are burning fiercely.

"What's happening?" I ask Harvey and McSween, who are standing in the hall outside the parlor.

"They poured coal oil over the woodpile at the back and set it alight," Harvey replies nervously.

"It's spreading slowly because of the adobe walls," McSween explains, "but the fire's got a firm grip. It's only a matter of time."

"So we're stuck in a burning house, surrounded by gunmen intent on killing us and with no way to escape?" I ask angrily. Again Harvey nods despondently.

I'm struggling to control my rage at being trapped and having lost Coronado again, when a voice shouts from the parlor, "Mrs. McSween's coming back." McSween murmurs, "Thank God," under his breath and opens the door. Susan McSween bursts through and embraces her husband.

Harvey and I stand by awkwardly as the McSweens each say how glad they are that the other is unharmed. Others, including Bill, are gathering in the hall behind us.

"We must surrender," Susan McSween declares to us all. "Colonel Dudley cannot help us, but he has offered all of us safe passage out of the house."

My heart leaps. Maybe it's all over, but then Bill speaks up. "Of course Dudley won't help us. He's part of Dolan's gang."

"He has to be neutral," Mrs. McSween says.

"Then why," Bill asks sarcastically, "are the howitzer and the Gatling gun pointing at us and not the Dolan store?" There's a murmur of agreement among the other men. "And what will Dudley do if we do surrender?" Bill goes on. "Hand us over to Dolan and Peppin?"

"He has to," Mrs. McSween explains. "He has no legal authority. The judge has to decide what's to be done."

Bill laughs bitterly. "The judge who's in the pay of the same men who support Dolan? Here's what'll happen boys." Bill turns to the Regulators. "If we surrender, those of us not taken behind the Dolan store and shot out of hand will end up in front of a judge who's been paid to hang us. Is that what we want?" A chorus of nos echoes down the hall. "Then we have to fight it out. If we can join up with the boys in the Tunstall store, there'll be at least thirty of us and—"

"There's only three left in the Tunstall store," Susan McSween interrupts in a strong voice. "Jesse Evans and his men moved in on them this morning. Most managed to slip out the back. The three who stayed held off Evans and the others, but they can't be any help. We're on our own in a house that's slowly burning down."

Bill curses under his breath but soon regains his confidence. "It don't matter. What's important is that we live to fight another day. The fire's moving slow, so we'll be all right until dark. Then we'll break out and head for the river. They'll never be able to follow us in the dark. We'll get back into the hills, regroup and do it proper next time. Finish the job afore Dudley can get here to give Dolan the advantage."

"There will be no next time." Susan McSween's voice is strong and commands the men's attention. "Don't you see that? This is the end. Dolan's won. Even if some of you escape, you'll be hunted down and finished off."

"We ain't finished off that easy, right, boys?" Shouts of agreement meet Bill's exhortation. "We're the Regulators. We can't fight the army, but we've got the beating of Evans and his scum. Right?" Another chorus of shouted agreement. "Who's with me for a breakout tonight?" The response from the Regulators is unanimous.

I look back at McSween, who is standing between his wife and Harvey, looking confused.

"You're all mad," Mrs. McSween says, shaking her head. "Come on, Alex. Let's get our things together." She steps forward, but her husband stays where his is as if rooted to the spot. "I don't know," he says miserably.

"What do you mean?" Susan asks, a puzzled expression crossing her face.

McSween looks terrified. His eyes are darting between his wife and Bill, and he's wringing his hands in front of him.

"I mean," he begins hesitantly. "I mean I have responsibilities. These are my men now that John and Dick are dead. I can't leave them."

"That's the way, Mr. McSween." Bill's voice is calm and encouraging. "You stick by us and we'll have your business back for you afore you know it."

"You shut up." Susan McSween's voice is hard and commanding. I spot Bill tense and his face distort into a black scowl. I silently pray he doesn't do something stupid. "Responsibilities!" Susan continues, turning to face her husband. "What about your responsibilities to me? Don't I count for more than this gunfighter trash you seem so fond of?"

"But they're my men," McSween says. "I can't abandon them. John had a dream. He wanted to start something good here. Something that wasn't the private preserve of some corrupt politicians and businessmen." As he talks, his hands settle and he calms down. "It's a good dream, and these trash, as you call them, and I are all that is left of John's dream. I have to keep trying as long as there's any chance of realizing the dream." Susan stares hard at her husband but says nothing. Everyone waits to see what will happen. Eventually, McSween continues. "You must leave, Susan. Dudley won't let any men come out unless we all do, but he will protect you. I'll come for you when all this is over."

I have a feeling like a black stone sinking in my stomach. The fighting will go on, and I'm still stuck in the middle. I angrily push past Bill and the others into the parlor and slump down in a tattered, dust-covered armchair.

I don't know how long I sit there, feeling sorry for myself. I hear shouting from other parts of the house, men come and go in the parlor, and occasional shots are exchanged through the windows. I ignore it all.

What I can't ignore is the increasing heat and the thick, dark smoke billowing into the room. Eventually, I can barely breathe, and I stumble across the hall and into the kitchen, where I find McSween, Susan and Harvey. I've heard both the McSween's voices raised as they argued back and forth about what is to be done, but the quarrel seems to be over now. Susan stands by the stove, her arms crossed, and McSween sits at the table, slouched forward with his head in his hands. Harvey sits beside him.

"You are a fool, Alex McSween," Susan says. "I have always admired your loyalty, but it is misplaced in this case."

McSween says nothing, and I am wondering whether I should say anything, when a shout of "Soldiers!" comes from the hall. Susan heads through and I follow.

The front door is open, and through it we see three soldiers escorting a small group of women and children along the street. The firing has stopped to allow them to pass.

"Will you give me safe passage if I join you?" Susan shouts, stepping out onto the verandah.

"I shall," the sergeant with the group replies, "but be quick."

Susan retreats to the kitchen. I step out the door.

"Be careful," the sergeant shouts. "I have orders to collect only women and children. I cannot protect you."

"I know," I say. "Is Lieutenant Fowler of the Tenth with you over there?"

"No. His troop was not back from the reservation when we left the fort this morning."

"If he arrives, could you tell him that Jim Doolen is here?"

"I'll do that."

Susan reappears. Without looking back, she strides down the path and joins the small group who set off down the street. I watch despondently until a bullet whines overhead and forces me back inside. The hope that I could get word to Lieutenant Fowler was my last chance for escape. Now I'm just another helpless pawn in whatever plan Bill has hatched to get us out before the fire destroys the house.

There are sixteen of us crammed into the kitchen, the only habitable room left in the slowly burning house: eight Hispanics who came with Jose Chavez, including the old man from La Luz; five Regulators, including Bill; McSween; Harvey; and myself. Night has fallen. It's moonless, but outside it's lit as bright as day by the flames from the burning house. Shadowy figures move about in the dancing light and occasional bullets thud into the adobe walls. I'm reminded of the vivid pictures of scenes from hell in the big illustrated bible in which my mother wrote the major family events.

The firing has almost ceased. Not only is it difficult to find targets, but it's obvious that we can't last much longer in what's left of the house. All Dolan and his men have to do is wait. We'll come to them. How we do that is up to Bill.

"Anyone feel like a song?" The closer we get to our bid for freedom, the more excitable Bill has become, singing and dancing wildly around the cramped room. It's almost as if he draws energy from our increasingly dangerous plight.

"We need to go," McSween says.

"We'll dance our way out, right past Dolan, Peppin and the rest." Bill grins broadly. "Here's how we'll do it. I'll take a group over toward the store. That'll draw the fire. The rest of you break out the other way and head down to the river. Who's with me?"

Jim French, who was part of the group who ambushed Sheriff Brady; Jose Chavez; and a new Regulator that I only know as Tom, immediately push forward to stand by Bill. Surprisingly, Harvey joins them.

Should I join them as well? The first group might have the element of surprise, but it's small and will be the focus of all the guns outside. When the second group breaks out, the gunmen around us will be distracted, but it's a much bigger group.

Before I can make up my mind, Bill goes on.

"Good. The five of us will go like bats out of hell when I give the word. Mr. McSween, you lead everyone else in the opposite direction. As soon as you're away from the firelight, scatter and try to make it down to the river. Clear?" There's a murmur of agreement. "Good. Then check your guns and let's get going."

Automatically, I check that my Cavalry Colt is loaded and ready. Then I step over to Harvey.

"You sure you want to go with Bill's group?" I ask. "You'll be drawing a lot of fire, and you don't even have a gun."

Harvey shrugs.

"Never was much of a shot. I'll keep my head down and hope for the best."

"Good luck," I say and turn away, but Harvey clutches at my arm. He's trying desperately to appear brave and nonchalant in front of the others, but I can see in his eyes that he's terrified. There are beads of sweat on his forehead.

"I'll tell you one thing though," he says with a weak smile, "if I get out of this, consumption or no,

I'm heading back east to spend the rest of my life in a nice safe law office."

I nod and try to smile encouragingly. Suddenly, Bill is beside me.

"You don't want to come with us?" he asks with a broad smile.

"I'll take my chances with Mr. McSween's group," I reply.

"Not the sort of work you thought you were getting into when we met on the trail?"

"It's not," I agree, "and I'm out of it. If I live through tonight, I'm going up to Fort Stanton to work as a scout."

"Army ain't for me. If you get tired of taking orders, me and some of the boys are going to set this territory alight. There's plenty cattle and few fences, and good money to be made from those who don't ask too many questions."

"You're going to become a rustler? What happened to the idea of getting a grubstake and setting up your own ranch?"

Bill shrugs and laughs.

"Were never for me. Too much of my da in me, I reckon. Well, good luck, Canada Kid. Maybe we'll meet again one day."

"Maybe," I say, but I hope not. Bill has got me into a lot of trouble, and yet there's a part of him I'll miss. Not the cold-blooded killer who can shoot a man in the head without a second thought, but the charming kid who can sing and dance with the best of them.

"Okay," Bill says. The bustle in the kitchen ceases and people pay attention. "It's time. The five of us will head for the store. This is the order: Harvey, Jim French, Tom, Jose and me. Go hard, shoot at anything that moves and good luck.

"Mr. McSween, as soon as we draw their fire, you lead the rest out in the opposite direction." McSween nods uncertainly.

"Right." Bill throws open the door. It's as bright as day in the yard. "Go Harvey! Head for the gate."

Harvey glances back at me and smiles. Then he is gone. The others pile out after him. I push my way to the window and look out just as a fusillade of shots ring out.

Harvey makes it to the gate in a crouching run, bullets whining by him and kicking up dust at his feet. He's running fast when his head snaps back and he tumbles. Jim French jumps over his body, but Tom stops to check him while Chavez, holding a wound in his shoulder, and Bill pile past. In the flickering light,

I can see the dark blood pooling by Harvey's head. Tom gets up, fires off a couple of shots into the darkness and follows the others. They've given up the idea of going to the store and are sweeping around in a wide arc to where we are supposed to be heading. I lose them in the shadows.

Harvey's dead, but I don't have time to mourn. McSween, the two remaining Regulators and Chavez's men are piling out the door. I follow. The old man from La Luz is beside me.

"*Recuerde el Alamo*," he says to me with a smile. Remember the Alamo. I will. If I live.

The eleven of us in McSween's group rush around the corner of the house in the opposite direction from Bill. It's a mistake. There are Dolen men there, and they haven't been distracted by Bill's escape.

The first volley drops three of Chavez's men in a heap. The rest of us scatter in all directions, except for McSween, who stands frozen in the middle of the yard, illuminated by the blaze behind him.

I crash through a low fence and collapse, gasping, behind a pile of lumber.

"Didn't expect we'd meet again this soon." I roll over to see Bill lying beside me, grinning. A strange, unreal quiet has fallen over everything, a sharp contrast to the clamor of gunshots a moment ago. We stare back at McSween.

"You ready to give up?" a voice shouts from the darkness.

McSween drops the pistol he has been holding limply in his hand and spreads his arms wide. A figure stands up and walks toward him.

"That's Bob Beckwith," I hear Bill say as the figure enters the firelight. "He's the snake that shot me in the leg when we got Brady and Hindman. I been after him since then."

"No!" I yell as I realize what Bill's about to do. I'm too late. Bill's shot hits Beckwith in the right eyeball, killing him instantly. He drops at McSween's feet.

For what seems like an age, there's a shocked silence. McSween stares down at Beckwith. Then, his arms still held wide, he raises his head and stares around at the silent darkness. The volley of bullets tears into McSween's chest. He staggers two steps back and drops his arms to his side, before collapsing forward beside Beckwith.

"What'd you do that for?" I shout at Bill as ragged firing breaks out all around.

"Beckwith deserved it," Bill says casually.

"But Alex McSween didn't. Neither did Harvey, or any of the men who've died because of you." I'm swamped by anger. All my frustration at Bill and his callous self-interest boils over and I have my revolver cocked and pointed at Bill's head before I realize what I'm doing.

Bill only smiles at me, his hazel eyes twinkling in the firelight.

"You ain't going to shoot me, Jim," Bill says.

I want to shoot him, more than anything else in the world, but he's right. I'm not like him. I can't shoot a man in cold blood, however much I hate him. I release the hammer and lower my weapon.

"Till we meet again," Bill says. Then he's gone into the darkness.

I don't have time to think much about what has happened. A bullet chips the piece of lumber by my head, reminding me I need to keep running.

Holding myself low and keeping to the darkest shadows, I work my way to the riverbank. Behind me the shooting dies away and I begin to hear the excited shouts of the victorious Dolan men. The war's over, and I'm on the losing side.

At the river I see a crowd of figures, but I avoid them. I head south, around the edge of town and back up to the livery stable. There are men down here, drinking and dancing in the street, but I keep out of the way and no one pays me any attention.

I find Alita and Coronado and saddle them both. As I'm about to leave, the stable boy appears in the light of the lantern by the door, but a single look at my revolver and the grim look of determination on my face and he scuttles off into the darkness.

I lead the horses until I am well clear of town; then I mount Coronado and, leading Alita, I head slowly through the darkness to Fort Stanton and whatever a new life without Bill has to offer me.

JOHN WILSON is the author of thirty-one books for juveniles, teens and adults. His self-described "addiction to history" has resulted in many award-winning novels that bring the past alive for young readers. John spends significant portions of the year traveling across the country speaking in schools, leaving his audiences excited about our past. Learn more about John and his books at johnwilsonauthor.com.

The following is an excerpt from Volume One of
The Desert Legends Trilogy by **JOHN WILSON**.

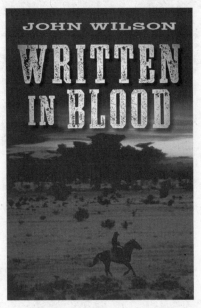

9781554692705 $12.95 PB

Set in the harsh desert world of the Arizona Territory and
northern Mexico during the 1870s, *Written in Blood*, the
first installment of the Desert Legends Trilogy, follows
young Jim Doolen as he attempts to find some trace of the
father who abandoned his family ten years earlier. As he travels
through a scorched landscape very different from the lush West
Coast forests of his home, Jim crosses paths with an assortment
of intriguing characters, including an Apache warrior, a cave-
dwelling mystic, an old Mexican revolutionary and a mysterious
cowboy. And with each encounter he learns something more of the
strange world he has entered and adds one more link in a chain
that leads back to his father—and back to a dark, violent past. As
his story approaches its thrilling conclusion in a ruined Mexican
hacienda, Jim comes to realize that his father's life was much
more complex than he had imagined, and that, in discovering his
past, he has opened the way to his future.

This is a world whose history is written in blood. Blood drenches the black dried scabs of the rocks, the rusty desert sands and the distant crimson mountains bathed in the dying light of the setting sun. It is the blood that has drained from conquistadores, Apaches, Mexicans, Americans, leaving their empty bodies to dry out in the unforgiving sun. Not for the first time, I wonder what the hell I'm doing here on this fool's errand.

I am camped on the edge of an eroded bluff of black volcanic rock. The only sounds are the quiet chomping of my tethered horse eating the nearby clumps of grass sprouting from cracks in the rock and the sizzle of the skinned jackrabbit on the stick over the crackling fire in front of me. The sky above is the deepest black I have ever seen and the stars so bright and close I feel I could reach out and pluck them.

I stare over my fire to the west, across the desert plain I crossed today, at the barely discernable black outline of the mountains where I camped last night. The tiny flickering campfire out on the plain is the only light. Every night for the past five days I have seen this fire as darkness falls. There is probably a man sitting by it looking up at the light of my fire. Who is he? Perhaps he is simply a traveler, taking the same route as I, but the loneliness of this place makes me think not. What his purpose is, I cannot guess. All I know is that every evening his campfire is a little closer.

I chose this place to camp because these low hills command a view of the way I have come, because there are some stunted trees for shelter should the clouds I saw building at twilight turn into a storm, and because there is a nearby spring for fresh water. It's a good spot, but it's not the land I have left.

Three months ago, on my sixteenth birthday, I was leaning on the rail of the schooner *Robert Boswell*, watching porpoises leap around us as we tacked across the Strait of Georgia toward the Strait of Juan de Fuca and the Pacific Ocean. My world then was blue—the dark blue of the water below, the pale blue of the sky above and blue-gray of the mountains at my back. I have not seen blue since I stepped off the ship in San Diego and launched myself into this land of rusty brown, burnt ocher and blood. The eternal snow on the peaks of the mountains back home is merely the memory of a dream.

My thoughts drift back to the modest parlor of the stopping house in Yale that my parents built in 1859 with gold my father had clawed from the Fraser River. I was born two years later, by which time business was booming as thousands of hopeful miners flooded through Yale on their way to the goldfields of the Cariboo, nursing their dreams of untold wealth.

I remember my mother telling me, "Your father found gold in the Fraser River, but we made a lot more money from the fools going to look for gold in the Cariboo."

My father came up from California to look for gold in the District of New Caledonia in May of '58. By the time New Caledonia became British Columbia later that year, he had staked and was working three good claims near Yale. Before a year was out, he had sold them, met and married my mother and bought the lot where our stopping house was to stand. But my father was not a man to let the grass grow beneath his feet. By the time British Columbia became the sixth province of Canada in 1871, he had been gone for four years.

I don't think my mother even resented my father leaving. I suspect she had known since they first laid eyes on each other that he would move on one day. He had what my mother called an impatient soul.

"Some folks just can't settle down in one place," she used to say. "They aren't made that way. With people like that you've got two choices: give up everything and accompany them, or accept that one day they'll be gone and enjoy the time that you are in the same place with them.

"Your father gave me two very precious things when he left me the stopping house: financial security and independence. Both of them are great rarities for women, and I wasn't about to give them up easily. And then there was you. I knew you'd leave one day too. I saw your father's restless spirit in your eyes the day you were born, but even a rambler needs roots and a strong foundation. I stayed and ran the stopping house to give you that."

On the last day before I left, my mother and I stood on opposite sides of the polished oak table in the parlor. She looked sad but not angry or tearful.

"Well, James, if you're heart-set on going, all I can do is wish you luck and give you this." She handed me a tin box that I knew well. I set it on the table, undid the latch and lifted the lid. Inside, Dad's Colt Pocket revolver lay nestled in a bed of worn red felt. Beside it was a powder horn, a bullet mold, a box of percussion caps and a collection of lead bullets. It's an old gun; you have to load each of the six chambers individually with powder, shot and percussion cap; but my father always said that was no disadvantage over the new fancy revolvers that took the ready-made cartridges.

"A handgun's only good for shooting at something closer than a hundred feet away," he used to say. "If you're that close to a man and you need more than one or two shots, you're probably already dead."

I practiced with the revolver until I became a pretty good shot, and I feel comfortable knowing that it's lying with my saddlebags across the fire from me.

"Won't you need it once I'm gone?" I asked my mother when she gave me the gun.

"No use for a gun here now," she said with a smile. "This is 1877. When your father first came up here, it was a different matter. There were a lot of rough characters coming through then and not much law to control them, but all that's changed. We've got laws and government now. A lady doesn't have need of a handgun here, but you may where you're going."

"I have to go and find out what happened to Dad," I said. "I always said I would as soon as I was old enough and able. I'll be sixteen in three days and I've got some money saved, so there's no point in waiting."

Mother nodded slowly. "When you make up your mind, nothing changes it. You're stubborn, just like him. He kept his thoughts close to himself, but once his mind was made up, God Almighty himself couldn't change it. I know I can't stop you going but, remember, you may not find him. He told me he was going to Mexico, but Mexico's a big place. Besides, he may not wish to be found or," she hesitated, "something may have happened to him."

"That's true, but somewhere down there, someone knows where he is or what happened to him, and I aim to find that out."

"Even if you find him," mother said thoughtfully, "he may not be what you expect. You were only six years old when he left, and he'll be forty-five by now. What do you remember about him?"

"I can see him like it was yesterday, not tall but strong. He could lift me like I was a feather. His hair was dark, but I was always fascinated by how red it was at the ends, especially his mustache where it dropped down the sides of his mouth. When I was little, I always thought he grew that mustache to try and pull down the edges of the smile he always wore.

"I remember him teaching me Spanish and telling me stories. He told me about the vaqueros and Spanish grandees in Mexico, the wild Apache Indians and cowboys in Arizona and New Mexico, and the gold prospectors and gamblers in California. I promised myself that I would go and see these places for myself one day."

"He was a good storyteller," mother said wistfully. "But there was a lot about his life before I met him that he never did tell, and God knows I asked often enough. For all his talk and tales, he was a secretive man, never wanted anyone to really know him. I wondered sometimes if he had something dark in his past that he was running from. He used to have nightmares, you know. I'd wake to find him sitting in the bed beside me, bathed in sweat, his eyes wide and staring as if the room was full of ghosts. I used to ask what he saw in the night, but he never told me. Always passed it off as something he ate for supper that disagreed with him."

"I didn't know."

"No reason for you to know. Mostly they were in the years after I first met him. They eased off after we got the stopping house set up and running, but they came back in the months before he left. I guess what I'm trying to say is that there was more to your father than the stories he told. You might be disappointed when you meet him."

I opened my mouth to protest, but Mother went on. "I'm not trying to talk you out of going. I know you've got his obsessions, and nothing I can say will change that. I just want you to go down there with your eyes open, because, even if all his stories were true, things have changed. It's not the world he knew down there twenty years ago. There are cattlemen, cowboys and gunfighters moving in there now. Civilization's creeping in, but it's a slow, violent process."

"But I have to try," I repeated.

"I know, and I've tried to give you the best tools I can. You're a fair shot with that revolver, you can at least stay on the back of a horse, and I've encouraged you to keep up with the Spanish he taught you. I also hope I've given you the sense to know when to stand and fight and when to run. So I guess all that's left is to wish you luck."

We embraced, and the next morning at daybreak I was gone to New Westminster to catch *the Robert Boswell.*

THE DESERT LEGENDS TRILOGY

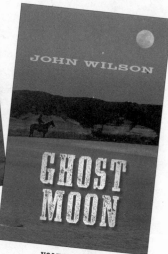

VOLUME ONE
Written in Blood
9781554692705
$12.95 pb

VOLUME TWO
Ghost Moon
9781554698790
$12.95 pb

COMING SOON

VOLUME THREE

VICTORIO'S WAR